MURDER ON CINNAMON STREET

A Shaky Detective Mystery

by

Lyla Fox

Copyright © 2013 by Lyla Fox

For information, email **Cozy Cat Press**, cozycatpress@aol.com or visit our website at: www.cozycatpress.com

COZY CAT
PRESS

ISBN: 978-1-939816-01-6
Printed in the United States of America

Cover design by Betsy Fox

1 2 3 4 5 6 7 8 9 10

*Dedicated to Betty Horvath, my very own Charlotte
A. Cavatica: A true friend and a good writer*

Also, enormous gratitude to The Arts Council of Greater
Kalamazoo for its faith in me and for twice awarding me its
Emerging Artist Grant, and to D & D Printing for always being
there for everyone

BEFORE

Only when she heard the door open, did she remember she'd forgotten to lock it. For a few seconds, the fear that accompanied her most of her life returned in a surge. Then she saw the figure in the doorway and relaxed. It was always good to see a friend. That's why the first blow caught her totally off-guard and sent her reeling. "Why?" was the question she struggled to utter before another blow rendered the answer irrelevant. Clara was dead.

Chapter One

All I wanted to do was stay there, in the overstuffed leather chair, and rest my aching feet. I had spent a long, frustrating day painting Marietta Stoll's house. The paint job and the pixilated Marietta, constantly questioning if I was using the yellow she ordered, had driven me half crazy. Yes, I assured her, the yellow—a ghastly color I tried to get her to reconsider—was indeed her choice. I knew I should be getting ready for the ladies, but I wanted just a few more seconds to myself. I'd earned the comfy chair and the ice cold soda.

Tonight I, Elizabeth Catherine (E to my friends) Clary, was hosting the monthly Literary Ladies Night, and the other two members Madge Bobik and Mignon Dalton, both well over forty years my senior, would soon appear.

"We have to get going, Howler," I said to my Heinz 59 mutt resting his extra long, extra droopy ears on the floor in front of the fire. My beloved pet, purchased at Animal Rescue four years ago when I was panic stricken and heartbroken, didn't look any more eager to rise from his comfy position than I was, but duty called.

And duty translates to Madge and Mignon. When my mother died the summer after I graduated with my MA in English lit from the University of Michigan, her death left me with nearly paralytic anxiety attacks and her two best friends. The born-elegant Mignon and the never-can-get-it-totally right Madge are as opposite as any two people can be, but they were, in a way, willed to me by my mother, and I'm stuck with them.

"Let's get the coffee started and find my copy of *The Circular Staircase,*" I said to Howler who grudgingly moved his bulky body, while retaining a bitter look in his soulful eyes. "Where is that darn book?" I finally found the vintage Rinehart mystery on the bottom shelf of the bookcase.

"E, there are all kinds of flashing lights down the street, didn't you see them?" Madge slammed through the front door with Mignon in her wake. "Don't you wonder what's going on?"

"Cool it!" Mignon snapped. "Were you born chasing ambulances?" She gracefully moved a strand of platinum hair away from her face. Tall and fine-boned, Mignon oozes elegance. Tonight she was wrapped in a mink guaranteed to piss off PETA. Her silken hair, pulled away from her face and turned down at her shoulders, made her appear decades younger. Though she never discusses it, I'm pretty sure she's on a first-name basis with all the best cosmetic surgeons in the Midwest.

Then there's Madge. She is an unmade bed. Over six-feet-tall, with hands and feet as large as most men's, her hair is a horrifying Morticia Addams black. I'd never say it to her face, but she looks like a retired female wrestler, with apologies to female wrestlers. The truth is that it was my mother who held them together and kept them from an all out knock down, drag out.

"Hey, you guys, there are cops down the street, and you sit like bumps on a log. Aren't either of you curious about what's going on?" Madge plopped onto the sofa as Mignon grimaced at her neighbor's less-than-eloquent way of phrasing things.

"She's exaggerating. One fire truck and one ambulance do not a crime scene make." Mignon slowly and aristocratically seated herself in the small chair that had been my mother's. "I have so been looking forward to this evening," she said. "I love our nights together."

Madge stared defiantly at Mignon. "And when do I get to pick?"

"When hell freezes over," Mignon said.

"Ladies, who wants what? I have coffee, tea, soda, and pinot noir." They weren't listening.

"Here we sit, bored and brain dead," Madge said, pouting like a three-year-old.

"I'm sure it's nothing." I wasn't sure as I thought about the flashing lights and sirens. But I didn't want there to be even the remotest possibility that Madge might be right about something awful happening on our quiet street ruled by majestic old Victorians. After all, I hadn't stayed in dull, nothing-happening Camphor for my health. Yes, I had suffered a debilitating attack of fear of the big wide world, but wanted it to be my little secret. Except for the murder of Philbrook Hanson forty years ago, Camphor was probably the safest town in the world.

"E's right," Mignon said as I poured tea. "We can't go ambulance chasing. There's nothing we can do. We'll only be in the way."

"I can't believe you two!" Madge abruptly rose from the sofa. "Aren't you a bit curious about what's happening?"

"Curious, yes," Mignon said, "Idiot-curious? No. Let's just say that E and I have heads on our shoulders."

"There goes another siren! I'm going down there." Madge ignored Mignon as she grabbed her jacket. "I'll let you sissies know what happened."

"Brain dead." Mignon said under her breath. "She'll get herself killed one of these days."

"I think I'd better follow her," I said totally against my fraidy cat instincts. My panic disorder makes mountains out of molehills so chasing ambulances and police cars is against my nature, my better judgment, and every fiber of my autonomic nervous system. But left to her own devices, Madge would get herself into one big mess.

"Wait!" Mignon chased behind me. "I can't keep up with those long, skinny legs of yours."

It was cold and dark, but the ladies were right. There was definitely something going on down the street. I could smell smoke and see lights. Madge was so far ahead of us that she was a Sasquatch in the street lights. "Maybe we shouldn't be doing this." My legs had turned into Slinkies. And my heart beat with staccato rapidity. I knew when I stopped that I would feel the light-headedness that always accompanies travels from my comfort zone.

We neared the scene, and I saw that it was the Nagel house, owned for at least fifty years by the undeniably strangest family in Camphor. Though the senior Nagels had been dead for over a decade, their spinster daughter Clara still lived there, a stranger even to her neighbors. The house had become an eyesore with overgrown brush and peeling paint, its decrepit condition now irrelevant as it burned with savage fury.

"My word! It's a tinderbox." Mignon gasped. We stopped and stared at the firemen racing to put more hoses on the fire. Then we saw the ambulance that had pulled around to the back. Our Friday night mystery novel discussion had been eclipsed by the real thing. I hoped Clara had gotten out, but feared the ambulance, with its light ominously dark, signified an unhappy outcome.

"Madge!" Mignon shouted. "Get your big old self over here and away from those firemen."

"Oh it's awful," Madge said in a tone that suggested just the opposite. "See that ambulance. It's going to get the body—Clara's body."

I shuddered and struggled to keep my legs from going out from under me.

"There's Whitey!" Madge shouted. "Whitey, come here!"

Whitey Barnes makes my top ten least favorite people so I wasn't thrilled Madge was gesturing wildly for him. He's both a fireman and policeman, as well as an ex-classmate of mine at Camphor High. Whitey calls me way too often suggesting that we should go out. Even though weekends can sometimes get very long and lonely, they are never so bad that I would consider going out with him.

"Hi, E." Even in the dark, I could see he was giving me his best teeth-whitened smile while probably flexing a muscle or two. "We sure have a mess here don't we?"

"What happened? Is Clara really dead?" My voice echoed in my ears.

"Nothing I can talk about right now," he said, so full of himself that he quickly reminded me why I couldn't stand him. A little power with Whitey is a very dangerous thing.

"Whitey, I knew your mother, and she wouldn't be happy that you are being such an ass," Madge had him by his jacket collar. "Now tell us what you know."

Like a ten-year-old upbraided by a stern aunt, Whitey began to spill his guts. "Well, Mrs. Bobik, as you can see, the Nagel house is burning to the ground. We found rags at the back that had been dunked in gasoline."

"Do you think that poor Nagel woman killed herself? Started her own house on fire?" Mignon asked.

"Someone sure wanted us to think that," he went on. "Whoever did this was stopped by the person who was walking by when the fire started. That person also ran inside to help Clara, but it was too late. She was dead from multiple chops. Now she didn't chop herself to death, did she?" He looked around to make sure we had all received his intended shock factor.

As Whitey droned on, I noticed a person standing to his right. Even in the dim lighting, he bore a strong resemblance to someone I once knew.

But before I could get close enough to see if the shadow was who I hoped he was, lightheadedness and fear engulfed me. I had to get out of there immediately. "Let's go. There's nothing more here," I told the ladies. If I didn't get back to safety quickly, I knew I would die or go crazy.

"Are you all right, dear?" Mignon took my arm as if I were the old lady and she the younger one. I hated the damn panic.

"I'm fine." I was already ahead of them. "I think this murder business is so awful, though, don't you?" *Breathe in two, three, four, out two, three, four.* My body and mind seemed to be in two separate places.

Predictably, the ladies forgot about me and returned to their petty bickering all the way to my house.

"Now," I said, feeling the welcome flood of relief that always accompanies my return home, "let's have some decaf." I poured the coffee and searched the book for a place to begin the discussion. "Let's forget Clara for a bit and talk about *The Circular Staircase.*" My breathing was becoming more even.

"She really must have been whacked away at." Madge said. "Who do you think slashed her to death?"

"My gawd," Mignon's face was as white as her hair. "Does that trash mind of yours never stop?"

"You know you're curious, too." Madge pointed a blood red fingernail at Mignon. "The murderer could still be around here. It might even be a neighbor."

"Ladies! Let's have a sweet roll." I nervously pulled open the package of homemade cinnamon rolls I had picked up on my way home from painting Marietta's

house. "We'll find out soon enough what happened."
My face still tingled from the awfulness down the
street. Though I hated to admit it, the ladies were right.
The murderer could be in the neighborhood.

"Good roll," Madge said with particles of the sweet
roll dotting her lips. "Where'd you get them?"

"Wipe your mouth please." Mignon dabbed crumbs
from her own mouth with one of the left-over birthday
napkins I'd set out. "E, before we get to the book—and
I really don't want to do that tonight too much has
happened. Tell us about your love life."

"Nice try," I smiled, "but you're on a need-to-know
basis where that is concerned, and you don't need to
know."

"Well, you aren't getting any younger. Duane and
me was married for eight years by your age," Madge
said, only half teasing.

"Duane and you were married," Mignon corrected.

"That's what I said." Madge stared back defiantly.
"E's thirty, and that means her chances are getting
slimmer."

"Hey, I'm only twenty-nine," I was surprised that I
felt defensive. Usually hearing the ladies chatter about
my love life, or lack thereof, was funny.

"And you are lithe and radiantly beautiful," Mignon
said. "It's just that we always hoped that you and John
Kidston would find your way to each other."

"That's old news," I knew I sounded more defensive
than I meant to.

"Now he's married to that absolute witch of a
woman." Madge popped another too-big section of
sweet roll into her mouth.

"I agree with Madge for once," Mignon said.
"Caroline Kidston is a positive nightmare of a woman."

I do admit to a certain amount of guilt where John's
marriage is concerned. After my last turn-down of his

proposal, at my mother's funeral of all places, he seemed to leap into marriage with a woman he met during his last year of law school at Michigan. Caroline Dartmoor Kidston was Vogue-cover beautiful and universally hated in Camphor. *Snob* and *cold* were the two words that accompanied any mention of her name.

"Let's change the subject." I was getting tired and knew that I had Maurice Brunson's enormous dining room to paint on Monday. It would be a challenging job, with its centennial ceilings and walls. I still had to get the paint and organize myself. It had taken a year for me to get John Kidston out of my thoughts. I wasn't going to let the ladies' discussion of him invite him back in. "Are we going to talk about this book or not?"

"I got to tell you," Madge's eyes were as big as her hair, "I didn't read it. You are picking books that are so boring. Did people live like that—money everywhere and all those manners?"

"I'm sure they didn't in your house," Mignon said with uncharacteristic meanness. I guess Clara's death had knocked us all off center. "I liked the book." She sniffed.

"Figures," Madge grumbled.

"Ladies, how about if we hold the book until next Friday? You need to get home and to bed." I knew next Friday would come, and we still wouldn't get to the book. Since we'd started Literary Ladies a year ago, we held three actual meetings and read one book— Madge's suggestion: *Harry Potter and the Chamber of Secrets*. I loved it. Mignon was insulted by Madge's choice.

"Ok." Madge said. "But I want to read this book I heard about at the grocery store. One of the clerks was talking about it—about a murderer who ran all over Chicago back in the day."

"Back in the day, huh?" Mignon sniffed. "You been hanging with your homies lately?"

"We'll talk about what book we do next Friday," I said, tired, scared, and angry with my mother for dying and leaving Heckl and Jeckyll with me. I looked around for Howler who needed to go out one more time and realized that my dog had given up the ghost and gone to bed.

"Good night, precious," Mignon said giving me a quick kiss on each cheek.

"See you soon," Madge hugged me, dwarfing my five feet nine. "Stay safe. Lock your doors after we leave."

I watched them throw barbs at each other as they got into Mignon's embarrassingly luxurious new Lincoln. She would drive them the three blocks down Cinnamon Street to houses right next door to each other.

"Coward," I said to Howler when he showed his whiskered muzzle as soon as the ladies left. "You're not fooling anyone. You show up for the food." I threw him half of the only sweet roll left, thanks to Madge's pugilistic appetite.

I poured myself a cup of coffee and flipped through my fandex to see what colors I needed to have mixed at Overton's Paints early Monday before I headed to Maurice's gothic wonder at the very end of Cinnamon. He wanted his dining room painted a deep, cathedral red found in Overton's custom Cambridge Collection titled Canterbury Red. The color was Maurice, classy but out-of-the-ordinary. He and I would both be glad to get rid of the last painter's dab at creativity, a brutish green that cast a pall over the whole room.

I called Howler in from my fenced in backyard where he'd said goodnight to several of my trees in his own special way.

When I crawled into the antique double bed that had been mine for most of my life, I tried to keep thinking paint colors. But as it always does when I'm alone in the dark, my mind submitted to thoughts that sent my heart racing, ominous thoughts of a murdered Clara Nagel and images of a hatchet wielding maniac. I shut my eyes tightly, trying to divert my catastrophizing. Gently, I pushed Howler back to his side of the bed, and suddenly recalled the handsome figure that I'd seen standing next to Whitey. *Please let it be who I think it is,* was the last thought I remember having before I went to sleep.

Chapter Two

Monday came way too fast. I hadn't gotten to the writing I had intended to do over the weekend. But I was increasingly losing faith that I would ever write anything of major proportion that would sell. Saturday and Sunday I left my laptop unopened and resorted to drinking way too many sodas and watching way too many old movies. "My dear, you'll never keep your shape drinking all that sugar." If I'd heard my mother say it once, I'd heard it a hundred times and had run away to school in Ann Arbor to stop hearing it. Now, I admitted to being willing to trade anything if I could have her there to chastise me for not being lady enough, not being fashionable enough. Looking in the mirror, though, I thought my mother might be delighted that my face had lost its round, little girl look and had taken on what my friend Earlene calls fresh-scrubbed, all-American girl look, whatever that is.

"How do you like this?" Steve Overton, owner of the paint store, had matched the color of red perfectly. "Maurice is a nice guy but I don't want to tick him off by giving him a red he doesn't like. He still complains about that shade of green every time he comes in here—even though he picked it out, or at least his crazy decorator did."

"I know." My free-floating anxiety is always worse at the beginning of the day so I was eager to get my business done and get to work at Maurice's.

"Did you hear any more about Clara Nagel?" Steve asked as he was ringing up the paint. "I heard it was murder. My dad and Harvey are poker buddies, and Harvey blabbed at Friday night's game."

Harvey was Whitey's uncle, Harvey Barnes, our town's chief of police and the one who appointed his nephew as assistant police chief. He was an older, more political, and barely more competent Whitey. "Did he say how she died?" I didn't want to know but couldn't help asking.

"Hatchet." He gave a quick shudder. "Someone really went to town on her. I guess there were pieces of her everywhere. They haven't found the weapon, though. I guess they don't have much to go on."

He lost me on the words *hatchet* and *pieces*. As he continued to describe the murder in bloody blow by hatchet blow detail, I felt an increasing need to escape. As he continued his graphic description of Clara's last moments, my legs and arms went numb. Time to leave.

"Thanks for the paint," I said in a non-sequitur so startling that I left Steve in wide-eyed confusion. "I'll probably need more. It's a big room and red is a hard color to get right."

"Bye," I heard him say, his voice ringing puzzlement.

Thank god for Maurice Brunson. I knew he'd take me a million miles from murder and mayhem to the giddy, fanciful land where he lived, full of gossip, extravagance, and frivolity. Maurice is one of the famous Brunson Spice Brunsons and a cousin to the president of the spice company. Maurice's predilections, however, led him to collect art and separate himself from the world-famous spice company that put our little town on the map and keeps most of Camphor employed.

"Well, here is the gorgeous Elizabeth Catherine Clary." Even though it was well past ten, Maurice greeted me in a green silk dressing gown with his long white-blond hair pulled back in a ponytail. "I am so eager to get this done. Doesn't it just thrill you to think of the possibilities that rooms offer?"

Good old Maurice. Watching his hands gesture dramatically and his little bird legs prance through the house as he ushered me to the dining room, I was glad he was rich enough to be sent to private schools. Public school playgrounds would have made mincemeat of little Maurice.

"Now, my darling," he said, "are we still sure that we want this red? I've been thinking that maybe a deep purple would be more satisfying?"

"No, I think you've made a great choice," I said. "We don't need this beautiful place to look like a bordello. I think purple might have that effect."

"You're probably right," he laughed. "Well, I had better get back to my guest," he winked. "Martha is here and will be able to get you anything you need. Byedy Bye." He trotted off as his housekeeper walked in with a robust cup of coffee for me.

"Turribel thing about that Nagel girl," Martha said handing me the coffee. "My family worked for the Nagels for years, and my brother Willie did her yard work. Horrible way to die."

I started unloading equipment as Martha talked. "What have you heard?" I asked, against all better judgment.

"Nothing really, except that they's sayin' it probably was murder. Murder! Can you imagine that! What's this world coming to when you can't be safe on the nicest street in town. I be havin' trouble sleeping at night."

"Me, too." Martha was old and sweet and had been with the Brunson family forever. She'd worked for Maurice's parents when she was young, and when they'd died, she stayed on to take care of their terminally bachelor son.

"Well, I'd better be getting back to the kitchen, Mr. Maurice says it's a good thing that young man reported the fire."

Then I remembered the dark, good-looking man standing near Whitey. "Do you know who he is?" Even in the midst of a tragedy I wasn't above checking out a hot guy.

"I do. Remember the gardener George Esqueda? Well, his son be back from the Air Force and has turned his dad's business into a landscaping one. He'll be here later today, and I jus' bet Mr. Brunson will have some questions for him, don't you?"

So I was right. It was Jory Escueda. There wasn't a girl my age who wouldn't remember the dark-eyed bad boy who set records for football and truancy. More than once I'd wondered what happened to him. My heart beat rapidly, and this time an unforgettable face, not panic, was the cause.

Much as I'd like to have taken a few more minutes talking about Jory, I needed to get busy and was soon preparing the trim and walls. The ceiling was in good shape and wouldn't require more than a coat of primer before I got to the real work. I'd picked out a luscious creamy white with a hint of gray for the trim so I was eager to get started. And if I was lucky, preparing and priming the trim would keep me there long enough to see Jory if and when he showed up. I hadn't seen him for at least a decade and if I was very, very lucky, he wouldn't have aged well.

As I patched the walls, I thought about the book I'd begun and rewritten for the past few years. No matter how hard I struggled to make it compelling, it wasn't. And I hated the thought that I was again at page fifty of a book I wouldn't finish. What a waste my MFA in writing was. Maybe my escape to painting was, as my mother complained, "Another excuse to avoid the real world of what real women do." In my mother's world, real women got married and had babies. Maybe I was more in love with being a writer than I loved writing. I hoped not.

What was it about painting people's houses that made more sense than anything else? Perhaps it was that I could control it, and I got out of my house and with people. My twenty-ninth birthday was a little over a month away, making me nervous and a bit embarrassed that I hadn't progressed further. My college roommate Suzi was the creative director of a Chicago ad agency, and my best friend from high school, Earlene Banks, was one of Michigan's best criminal defense attorneys. Here I was painting people's houses and babysitting two septuagenarians. E Clary, this is your life!

What a whiner I was becoming. I gave myself a mental slap and turned to Clara, a truly pitiable person. The generally accepted story about her went like this: her parents, like mine, had her very late in life after a great many miscarriages. And, like me, she was overprotected and socially awkward. When Clara was sixteen, her parents had very uncharacteristically gone to a convention in Detroit which her father, as head of accounting at Brunson Spice, had been required to attend. Their housekeeper and her daughter, Clara's age, had stayed with Clara that weekend. The housekeeper, always sympathetic to Clara's sad situation, let the privately-tutored Clara go to a school dance with her daughter who promised to look after Clara. Several hours later, the housekeeper's daughter returned frantic that Clara had disappeared with a young man she'd met at the dance. The Nagels were called home, and two days later Clara was found in a motel in Grand Rapids with a young man she'd met at the dance. The young man was given a tidy sum of money to disappear and Clara was seen very infrequently after that and always in the company of her parents.

Now Clara Nagel was dead. Chills went from my ears to my toenails.

"E, come join me! Let's eat." Maurice's voice trilled from the kitchen to the dining room where I had finished preparing the trim and one wall.

One of the best parts of working for Maurice is lunch. Martha always creates mouth-watering food. Today it was shrimp and avocado salad with a low-calorie lemon and olive oil vinaigrette. In the center of the table was a plate of her signature homemade cornbread muffins with honey butter. Yum!

"Let's talk about that awful business at the other end of the street." Maurice delicately poked small bits of salad with his fork. "That girl never had one minute of joy, and now she's dead. And you know it's only the second murder ever recorded here in Leave-It-To-Beaverland."

"Steve at the paint store said she'd been stabbed again and again."

"A nightmare," he said taking another bite of his salad. "Horace will be very bothered by this."

"Sorry, Maurice, I can't figure why Clara's death would be a blow to Horace. I know her dad was the Brunson Spice accountant, but how does that connect Horace Brunson to Clara?"

"Horace is Clara's godfather," Maurice volunteered. "And he manages her estate. Mind you Horace and I don't do much confiding in each other—stodgy old fart that he is—but it's almost public knowledge that there are a few legal matters he still engages in—the Nagel estate is one of them."

"Horace is their lawyer? Why isn't the estate handled by Randall and John Kidston? They handle everything else. And Horace is president of Brunson Spice. How would he have time to deal with the Nagels?"

"Simmer down, my sweet young friend. Horace has a Yale law degree, you know. Like the rest of us, he's a Yalie, but he was also possessed of an ambition that most of the Brunsons left to the bourgeois. He got a law degree and took the bar lest all the Brunson billions go down the drain. Thank god that has never happened or the rest of us philanderers would be in mucho shitto," he laughed.

"But I'm still not sure why Horace would take such an interest in Clara."

"Horace and his wife Amelia had only one child, a son. I think they liked the idea of having a girl in their life. They got Clara lavish presents for her birthday and Christmas. Who knows why they took such an interest in a dull, uninspired child. But they did. You know Clara was a major stockholder in Brunson thanks to Horace and her parents."

"And she never went anywhere or did anything."

"Never." He sipped the hot mint tea Martha had poured for us. "Now tell me what you'll be doing for Thanksgiving."

Until he mentioned it, I hadn't remembered that Thanksgiving was bearing down on me—only a few weeks away. "I'll be doing the usual. Mignon will probably go east to her cousin Vi's, and Madge and I will have turkey and all the fixings at my house." I'm not a bad cook, but I usually eat Lean Cuisine or a quick-fix meal that Rachael Ray directs me to.

"You know I haven't seen Vi Brunson Thornton for years. She's a distant cousin of mine, too. Mignon and I used to be great pals until she got so goddamned snooty. You know, young lady, there was a day when Mignon Dalton could down whiskey sours with the best of us."

"Maurice! I can't believe you said that!" I nearly choked on a piece of avocado. "Mignon would not be happy to know you're talking about her behind her back."

"Oh, I've said worse to her face. Now if you'll excuse me, I have a pedicure to get to. How's the dining room coming?"

"It's coming, but we'll have to do two coats unless you want it to be fire engine orange."

"Oh, gawd no! When I play fireman, I do it a different way." He gave me an unmistakably lascivious wink and left for Peg's Pamper Palace where Maurice, Mignon and all the rest of Camphor's elite spent hours getting their nails polished and their lips waxed and plumped.

I returned to painting. The ladies incessantly urge me to change jobs—to get a respectable job is the way they put it. They don't get what it is about painting that keeps me happy. I don't either really. In my head I've started at least three novels that would make Dr. Combs, my favorite writing teacher at Michigan, proud. That I had not yet finished any of them would not, however, delight him.

In what seemed a matter of seconds, the hands on the large grandfather clock in the dining room went from a little past noon to two. I was thinking I might get the first coat on the trim and ceiling before I left, when the doorbell rang.

"Is Maurice Brunson here? We have a two o'clock appointment."

There he stood in all his radiant glory. Not only had Jory Escueda aged well, he sizzled the same sexuality that had attracted a three-years'-younger high school girl all those years ago.

"Tell him Mr. Brunson called to say he be a few minutes late," Martha shouted from the kitchen. "Miss E, would you take him to the den?"

"Elizabeth Clary?" Jory's volcanic eyes fixed on me. "You're little Elizabeth?" His smile was mega watt.

"I'm pretty much E now." I tried to smile but felt my upper lip twitch. "Here's the den. Maurice had an appointment downtown, but he should be right along," I sounded like someone practicing English as a second language.

"Thanks. You are all grown up, E." He said it as if it was a very good thing. "You were three years behind me, right?"

"Right." I was surprised he remembered.

"All arms and legs, but cute. Very cute."

"Oh." I had no words.

"I know your dad is gone, but is your mother still living in the big, beautiful house?"

"She died about four years ago." No smiling about that.

"I'm sorry to hear that. She was always very nice to me." He sat on the edge of the sofa. "You were too," he smiled. "I remember one hot day when I was doing yard work at your place. You brought me lemonade, and I thought 'what a sweet kid.'"

Not so sweet. I used every excuse I could to be around him. "And your parents?"

"My dad died last year. He'd been in assisted living for a year or so after his stroke. My mama's still alive. That's why I'm back. Can't let the family business go to sod." He waited for my response then added. "That's a joke, E. Let a lawn business go to sod."

"Funny." I smiled and had absolutely nothing else to ask him that could be considered remotely rational.

"Where did you go when you left Camphor?" That was my best effort.

"Prison."

"Oh."

"E, I'm kidding, though I think there are those that kind of expected me to head there. I was kind of a mess in high school. The Air Force changed all that. They put me through school, and now they're helping me through law school. I'm still in the reserves."

"Good for you." It sounded so condescending that I wanted to shake myself.

"I'm staying with my mother over on Cayenne Street until my own place is ready."

"I remember that you Esquedas were a big family." Big, smart, and hardworking—were the deets on the family.

"There are four of us kids. I'm second to the oldest. My older sister is a doctor in California; my younger brother is at the Air Force Academy, and my little sister Lucy is a nurse practitioner here at the hospital."

"I know her! She works with Dr. Newell. Her name is Lucy Rodriguez. She's beautiful."

"Lucy married Javier Rodriguez two summers ago. He's in the state police, stationed ten miles away. They have a one-year-old named Lupe who is the apple of my eye."

The more he talked, the more I wished I could be the apple of his eye. Thank you, Maurice, for not getting back any sooner.

I counted my blessings too soon. Maurice's voice with its lilted tone could be heard from the hallway. "I'll be right there, darlings."

"E, thank you for keeping Mr. Esqueda company." Maurice made a grand entrance, directing his words to me, but his eyes didn't leave Jory. "I understand you've brought some plans to show me."

"Hello, Mr. Brunson." Jory put out his hand in an all-business greeting signaling the older man that he was all-business and not interested in any other activity Maurice might suggest.

I excused myself and returned to painting, thinking alternately about Clara Nagel's murder and whether or not the very alluring Mr. Esqueda was spoken for. My unrelenting interest in the latter told me that it had been far too long between dates.

My cell phone rang just as I was beginning the first coat of primer.

"E?" the voice on the other end was quickly identifiable. "I'm hoping you can stop by the house sometime this week. Caroline is eager to have you do some painting for us."

"I'm tied up at Maurice Brunson's until the end of the week, John," I said to the man with whom I had been linked romantically from my senior year of high school through college. "How soon do you need the work done? I might be able to get over by the end of the week to discuss the details."

"That's great. We would like it done before the holidays. Caroline's father is coming, and she is eager to have the house looking presentable."

"I probably won't be able to have it done entirely, but I'll make it look acceptable." How much better did they need their five-star monstrosity to look? Caroline's father lived in Boston and was one of the most successful investment bankers in the country. He continually showered her, his only child, with gifts, and his wedding gift had been to totally refurbish and remodel the late Martha Brunson's estate on Clovelly, surely the most magnificent house in Camphor.

"How about if I call you and stop by sometime Friday to see what you want done?"

"Thanks, E," John said, his voice marking his genteel, well-schooled wealth and breeding. If only all he'd wanted was friendship. We'd still be best buddies.

I had just said goodbye to John when the hunky Jory gave me a casual wave as Maurice ushered him out the door. My heart beat a rapid march to my ears.

When I stopped painting at five, I was dead tired. I gathered all my paint paraphernalia together in a corner of the dining room until the next day before I poured my tired self into my four-year-old Toyota Truck and drove home. Howler would be more than a little glad to see me. I'd left him alone too long. I made a mental note to be sure to dash home the next day so I could have lunch with my dog.

The answering machine was flashing in the kitchen my mother had meticulously remodeled in French provincial. I'd spent many cold Michigan nights in front of its brick fireplace, drinking lattes and reading Jane Austen novels.

"Hey, boy!" I let the phone blink as I rubbed my dogs' ears and gave him kisses all over his smelly dog head. Then I gave him three doggie treats and let him out. Like most of us, Howler can be bought .

"Well, boy, any doings here today?" I couldn't take one more dastardly deed in my neighborhood.

"You have three messages," The machine told me.

"Hi, E, this is Earlene. I wondered if you want to go to a movie this weekend. Bryce is in San Antonio at a conference." It was Earlene Waters Banks, one of my closest friends in Camphor and the only one without an AARP card.

Earlene and I have been friends since middle school. She met her husband Bryce Banks her first year of law school in Detroit. Bryce, a science teacher at Camphor High, was working on his master's in physics at Wayne State, and they connected at a Democratic rally. Her practice keeps her so busy that I don't get to see her as often as I like. I made a mental note to call her back.

"Ok, roomy, what are you up to? I read about a murder in Camphor and my blood ran cold. Call me." My college roommate Suzi is a voracious reader and our Camphor hatchet job must have made news even in Chicago. From undergrad at Michigan, she went right into advertising and has been a star ever since.

Suzi and I work hard at unconditional love. She tolerates my neuroses, and I remind her that she's a lot better than her over-achieving husband makes her feel at times. Her husband is our only glitch. In my book Aaron is an elitist snob from Dartmouth's Tuck graduate school who sucks up to anyone who can further his favorite cause: himself. So far his plan has worked brilliantly, but to my knowledge, Suzi is the only one who can stand him.

"Elizabeth Clary, we need to go out." I hoped the voice was the one I wanted it to be. "This is Jory Esqueda, and I'm not letting my good fortune pass me by. We need to follow up today's meeting with a drink somewhere, don't you think?"

I did think. But I also wanted my hands to stop shaking before I tried to dial the number Jory had left. How long had it been? I hated to think my last date had been the fix-up Mignon had arranged with the young radiologist from Camphor General who she had promised would be "the man of your dreams" and who turned out to be someone who talked incessantly about himself, picked his teeth with a toothpick all through dinner, and on the drive home reached for every part of my anatomy before I bid him a very final farewell—translation: a swift kick to the shins.

My only semi-long term relationship in recent memory was a PhD candidate who was in Camphor to conduct a land study for Michigan State University and who showed an interest in continuing our relationship when he went back to East Lansing. For me, absence did not make the heart grow fonder.

The dry spell between Mr. Tooth Picker and this call from Jory had caused me to question my too-quick turndowns of John Kidston's proposals. Maybe love didn't have to be all tingly and glittery. Maybe for some of us it could be less passionate and more peaceful.

The glitch in my opting for satisfying rather than flammable is the story my mother told and retold of how my father had literally swept her off her feet when she was a senior at the University of Alabama, and he was a handsome Army officer stationed nearby. "It was love at first sight—totally and breathlessly," she said again and again. "Oh, E, hold on for that. You'll be so glad you did." At the time, she was nudging me toward John Kidston, but her story became my dream.

Jory Esqueda certainly wasn't love at first sight. What I felt for him as a freshman in high school was a frightening awakening that made me glad I was too young for him to look at. But there was no doubt there was something, even way back then.

"Jory? This is E Clary returning your call," I left the message on his machine and hoped he'd call back before I chickened out.

Like clockwork, the ladies were coming up the front steps when I went to check on the mail.

"We wondered if you wanted to go for a bite, dear," Mignon said as she rolled her eyes suggesting that she wasn't happy to have only Madge for a dinner companion.

"You know ordinarily I would," I said half-truthfully, "but I just got in from work, and I'm looking forward to an evening by the fire and working on my book." My book, an ephemeral entity at best, was the excuse the ladies could understand and accept. The concept of "me time" was lost on them.

"We had some great juicy news to tell you," Madge said, her black hair a severe contrast to her orange polar fleece jacket. "Well, I guess we could tell you here and now."

"Oh, phooey!" Mignon lost her patience. "We found out who pulled Clara Nagel from her burning house. Remember George Esqueda? Well, young George, I guess they call him Jory, was the one who happened to be walking by and saw the fire. He tried to save Clara."

They gave me a few far less interesting bits of news and then roared off in Madge's peppy Mazda Miata, leaving me to consider why ex-wild child Jory Esqueda appeared to be showing up way too often in way too short a time. Why had he been walking by Nagels? Suddenly dark and handsome was become dark, handsome, and mysterious.

When the phone rang, I continued working on my laptop and let it go to the machine. I heard Jory's voice asking me to call him back. I wasn't sure I would. Maybe what I had mistaken for signs of romantic promise was really a signal that danger was near. My hands shook as I held my breath against a wave of panic and wished that anyone but Jory Esqueda had pulled Clara Nagel's body from her burning house.

Chapter Three

I didn't return Jory's call. I did toss and turn most of the night thinking about him and woke feeling as though someone had used me for his or her personal punching bag. I made a mental note to get to bed very early that night.

Maurice was gone when I got to his place so I took the warm caramel latte Martha kindly offered and went to work. I would be done with this job by late Thursday night. Though I can't say I was thrilled about it, I would be able to connect with the Kidstons on Friday. I was slightly puzzled as to why Caroline Kidston, who had at least half a dozen interior designers at her beck and call, wanted me to do the work. Maybe it was all John's idea, and if so, that would make for a very awkward work environment.

While painting, I thought about the novel I was working on. No brilliant ideas popped into my mind to take it beyond the first fifty pages that sat on my roll top desk that had once been my father's. And at that moment, Clara Nagel's murder, which was growing in notoriety, was far more interesting than anything I'd written. The Detroit and Grand Rapids papers and television stations were all working up a lather as to why she'd been murdered and how likely it was that the murderer still lurked somewhere very near. It made safe and sound seem far, far away. And I was drinking more and more sugar-sweetened soft drinks to soothe my nerves—a paradox, of course. I noticed that morning that my jeans were fitting a little tighter than I liked. I better switch back to water with lemons floating in it if I didn't want to float up a size.

I looked out the window and noticed a figure working to make sure Maurice's prize rose bushes were ready for winter. I'd know that cute butt anywhere. Jory Esqueda was on the premises. I stopped mid paint stroke to watch him. The weather report for the next few days threatened the first snowstorm of the year so he probably recognized that time was of the essence. Time was important to me, too. I reluctantly turned from watching Jory's behind to continue painting. With the ceiling and trim painted and the walls holding a first coat, I was on track to meet my self-imposed deadline. Rid of the garish green, the room was taking on a regal look. How could I explain how satisfying I found restoring Cinnamon Street's gracious old lady to its previous grandeur? If I didn't know what made me feel so fulfilled and happy, there was no way I could articulate to others my reason for eschewing the life I was raised for to slap coats of paint on old walls.

I had at least one paint job a week through February so along with the tidy sum I inherited for doing nothing except become an orphan—still a point of guilt—I wouldn't have to fry burgers in the foreseeable future.

"Looks nice."

I hadn't heard Jory enter, but there he was drinking a glass of ice water and shooting his onyx eyes straight at me.

"I didn't hear you." I nearly dropped my roller.

"I move like a cat, a trick I learned while working undercover for the CIA."

"You worked for the CI….Oh, you're kidding." I felt silly. I'd fallen for his little joke hook, line and sinker.

"I'm kidding, and that wasn't very nice of me as trusting as you are."

He had the most amazingly handsome face, strong-boned with rounded corners. I found it hard to believe that any woman in her right mind could resist him.

"I got your call too late to call back." It sounded feeble. "I was going to call you when I got home today." I totally lied.

"That's ok. I just thought it might be fun to go for a drink."

"I'd like that." Forget why he'd been trawling near Clara Nagel's the night she died. This guy was worth a test drive, I rationalized.

"Well," he brightened, "that's good. How about around seven tonight? We could have a late dinner and get to know each other."

"Sure." How had a drink turned into dinner?

Jory returned to his work, and I painted with far more gusto than I'd had minutes before. About ten thirty I heard a siren race past Maurice's and knew that Whitey had managed to corner a speeder—probably someone going twenty-six in a twenty-five-mile-an-hour zone.

"It can't be taking him that long to get his business done," Martha had said when she brought me a glass of iced tea. Maurice walked through the door not long after I returned from a quick lunch with Howler—yogurt for me and Iams for him. We were both relieved to see him return.

"Martha was worried about you," I told him. "How do you like the paint?"

"Lovely," he said, a bit distracted. "I didn't mean to be gone so long but I had more work to do with the bank and then checked in with my financial advisor. Brunson is going through some changes, and I wanted to make sure my investments are sound."

I wondered what changes the spice company, Camphor's most essential employer, might be going through, but I didn't ask. I know at work to keep my questions to myself. Maurice wasn't offering any information, and I wasn't going to ask for any. Besides, I had something much more pleasant to think about: dinner with Jory.

No sooner had Maurice gone upstairs to get ready for his yoga lesson than John Kidston arrived with papers for him to sign. I don't see John often, and it's not that I pine for him, but given our history, I still feel awkward around him.

"Is Maurice here, E?" he asked when I opened the door after Martha shouted she had her hands in bread dough and couldn't get it.

"He went upstairs to dress. Do you want me to call to him?"

"No. I'll just leave the papers here. How have you been?"

John Kidston is very tall and thin. He's handsome in that old-movie-star-like-Gary Cooper way. Girls have always found him attractive with his polish and all-American wholesomeness. His wife Caroline is also extraordinarily good looking so the one kind thing people can say without qualification is that they are a lovely looking couple.

"I'm fine. Maurice has me painting these walls an unusual red. I like it, don't you? I was worried at first, but the more I see it, the better I like it. You don't think it's too much, do you? I mean, he hated the last color, and I don't want him to hate this." I stopped. Diarrhea of the mouth was a sure sign of my discomfort.

"It looks good. You look good too, E. How's the writing going?"

"Not well. I seem to be a better painter than writer." I was uneasy getting into personal conversation territory.

"E," Jory walked into the room, "I forgot to tell you to dress casually. We'll probably go to that micro brewery at the edge of town." He turned to see John.

"Jory, do you remember John Kidston?"

"You mean Johnny Kidston, JV right guard." He put out his hand eagerly to greet John who looked more puzzled than pleased. "John was a freshman on the JV team when I was a senior starter on varsity. You had good hands as I remember."

"Good memory. Well, tell Maurice to get those papers signed and have them back to me in—never mind, I'll give him a call." John left.

"Something I said?" Jory asked after John's abrupt departure.

"No," I tried to play it off, "something I did."

"Well, I'm back to work. Remember, dress very casually."

Or dress not at all. Jory oozed knowing how to handle women, and I knew I had better be careful or I would be putty in his experienced hands.

Maurice never reappeared so I finished most of the room and tidied up before I left. I told Martha I would be back the next day to complete the job, feeling pretty darn satisfied that it had gone so well and that I was way ahead of schedule.

I got home a little after five, and since Jory wasn't to appear until seven, I took my much-neglected pooch for a walk. "You have a very bad mama, don't you?" I said as I snapped on his leash. "Well, we're going to take a long walk and follow it with a huge bowl of dog food." I swear my dog understands words. He wagged his tail and jumped up and down as I struggled to untangle his leash.

It was bitter cold as we started down Cinnamon. I wished I'd put on more than my polar fleece. "You must be chilly, too," I said to Howler who was straining to race ahead to encounter smells, old and new. "Maybe I'll get out my sewing machine and make you one of those doggie jackets for Christmas, how about that? Then you'll be like all those silly movie star dogs. But you're too big to put in my purse." I wasn't kidding about making him a jacket. I had a yen to sew and other than making a couple of long, soft skirts last spring, I hadn't done much sewing. My fabulous Pfaff was the last big gift my mother bought me.

I'd intended to walk past Madge and Mignon's, but my conversation with Howler had thrown off my concentration, and I was instead at the corner of Cinnamon and Sage. I began to turn toward the other direction, but Howler pulled hard in the direction of the charred remnants of what only a few days ago had been the gothic, vine-entangled Nagel home.

No funeral for Clara was what people in the town reported. As per her wishes, she'd been buried next to her parents in the Episcopal cemetery. Word was that she had left a healthy chunk of her fortune to the library and another to a foundation for young girls.

Seeing the house gave me weak knees and shut off my circulation. Suddenly my hands and feet became very cold. If I believed in ghosts—and I'm not sure I don't—I'd worry that the tormented soul of Clara Nagel was swirling around. Why hadn't Harvey and Whitey found out anything? We were all sitting ducks until the murderer was apprehended.

"Come on, fellow. There's no need for us to hang around here." I tugged Howler away from the bush he was sniffing top to bottom. "Time to go."

As soon as we returned home, I fed Howler and still had an hour and a half until the charismatic and desirable Jory would appear. A warm bath full of sudsy goodness called to me.

I poured my favorite bath gel into the hot running water, grabbed the Oxford American magazine to which I am devoted and got ready for a leisurely soak. Paint and turpentine smells were replaced by rosewater and music from my bathroom radio. Lovely.

Howler was the first to hear it, and his barking was immediate and incessant. I started to tell him to calm down and then I heard it too—a kind of rustling. I jumped from the bathtub, grabbed my robe and opened the door. My dog, waiting frantically just outside, ran in. I locked the door and hoped I had locked the front door. Chances were I hadn't. Until the Nagel murder no one ever thought of locking doors. Camphor wasn't that kind of place.

The disruptive sounds continued. Someone was definitely in the house. Howler stood near the door of the large bathroom, his growl was menacing. I was headed toward a grand mal panic that renders me helpless and shoots me into another sphere. I could see and hear, but everything seemed hazy and disconnected. Was the person who murdered Clara now in my house? My eyes blurred and my ears rang. In a few seconds I would faint unless I got hold of myself.

"It will be ok, guy," I said to both Howler and to me. "Just calm down."

Things were being thrown around and broken. I heard glasses from the kitchen shatter and feared that most of my mother's Limoges was now history. That was small potatoes compared to what could happen to me if the person downstairs were truly Clara's murderer. I gently turned off the light and heard only Howler's threatening growl punctuated by my erratic breathing.

I wished to heaven that I had had the sense to install a phone in the bathroom. All I could do was wait and hope. Footsteps on the stairs. Oh god! The unwanted visitor was getting closer and closer. It could be the end of my life. That thought reverberated, and all I wanted to do was curl up and return to childhood and the two people who had always made me believe I would be safe. The steps were right outside the door. He knew I was there. The doorknob turned. Blackness.

A pounding on the door was my first sign that I wasn't dead, bludgeoned to death by the intruder. The wonderfully familiar voice was the second.

"E! E!" Madge shrieked, "Are you all right?"

"Yes," I said weakly, embarrassed by my lack of ability to stay conscious in times of stress. "Let me open the door."

As I rose to unlock the door, I realized that I had hit my head on the tub. Blood trickled down my cheek to my shoulder. "Just a minute," I grabbed a washcloth and pressed it tightly against the side of my head. I didn't want to scare her to death.

I opened the door to let a totally discombobulated Madge and a clearly unglued Mignon in.

"Is that siren coming here?" I was standing with only a bath towel around me.

"I called the police," Madge said pulling me to her. "What in the hell went on here? We came over to tell you about Horace Brunson and some person pushed past us and ran out your door. He had a mask on. Oh, E, we thought you were dead." Madge, who usually had nerves of steel, sobbed.

By the time Whitey arrived, Madge and Mignon were both crying.

Minutes later we were all sitting in the kitchen with Madge pouring freshly-brewed coffee as I tried to reconstruct the last hour for Whitey. It was then that Jory entered.

"Don't I know how to greet a person!" I tried to relax him but I could tell from his face he was nearly as shaken as the ladies. "Are you all right?" He stared at the bloody cloth I was holding against my head.

"I'm fine." Having changed into jeans and a sweater, I rose to stand next to him. Neither Madge nor Mignon seemed at all pleased to see him. "Madge Bobik and Mignon Dalton, this is George Esqueda's son Jory."

"George Junior, really, but my kid sister Lucy's George came out Jory. It stuck. Good to see you again," he smiled his wondrous smile.

Madge warmed immediately, but the look on Mignon's face told me that she was going to be a hard nut to crack.

"I'm going to take a look around," Whitey, apparently bored with a conversation not focused on him, rose from the table. "Seems like whoever it was had something specific he or she was looking for."

I hated to admit it even to myself, but I was so frightened that I was actually glad to have Whitey there. I was scared enough to think even incompetent Whitey might be able to handle things. I *had* been hit on the head.

"You said you came to tell me something about Horace Brunson." I suddenly remembered what the ladies said when they found me in the bathroom.

"Now is not the time." Mignon shot Madge a warning look.

"We'll talk about that later," Madge said contritely.

"Talk about what? Tell me what it was you came here to tell me." I was starting to panic again.

Whitey was back before we could continue the conversation. "We can't be too careful, E, You need to get someone to stay with you. After what happened to Clara Nagel and now to Horace Brunson we can't afford to take chances."

"What happened to Horace Brunson?" I knew the answer before I finished the question.

"He was found dead—murdered—about an hour ago in his office at the plant," Whitey said. "My Uncle Harvey's still at the crime scene."

"That's what we came to tell you," Madge said before I again fainted dead away.

Chapter Four

When I regained consciousness, I was on the floor of my kitchen, with someone calling my name. My head throbbed.

"E?" Jory held my hand and the ladies fanned me with dishcloths.

"E, wake up." Mignon said as I struggled to sit up. I couldn't remember a time in my life when I'd felt more helpless or stupid with Jory, Whitey, Mignon, and Madge staring at me. Dope, thy name is Elizabeth Catherine Clary.

"I'm getting you to the doctor." Jory put his arm around me to steady me as I stood.

"Not yet. I haven't finished questioning her." Whitey was his most official.

"She's bleeding and needs to see a doctor." Jory scooped me into his arms. After he gently placed me in his over-sized pickup and when he was driving me to Camphor General, he called his sister Lucy.

"She's going to meet us. Dr. Newell is already there," he told me.

I'd known Glen Newell since I was a kid. In fact, Madge and I think Glen and Mignon have a little thing going on, but neither of them will ever admit to it. In public, they act like they hate each other, but evidence points to the contrary. Sometimes Dr. Newell's big Buick is parked in front of her house all night. Because it's Mignon, and because Madge and I don't have a death wish, we have a strict don't ask/don't tell policy where Dr. Newell is concerned.

A young, very pretty Hispanic woman greeted us the minute we got inside the door.

"E, I think you know my sister Lucy." Jory's arm held me tightly. "Lucy, do you remember Elizabeth Clary?"

"I do." The woman's smile was as beautiful as her brother's. "I don't know if you remember, but when I was in ninth grade a bunch of senior girls were making fun of the way I accented some of my words. You walked up and told them they were just jealous because I was prettier than they were. They didn't like that, but I did. It's nice to get a chance to thank you."

"That was a very brave thing for me to do, wasn't it?" My laugh sounded hollow in my pounding head. "I'm not usually like that."

"Well, there you are." Glen Newell was in his scrubs, but his hair was still the same perfectly sculpted do, steel gray and sprayed back into an aging-movie star look. "I heard they'd brought you in."

"Did you know Horace Brunson was murdered?" I asked. I thought that since Glen had fixed most of my hurts since I was little, he would have a solution to the awful news that was probably at that moment racing through Camphor.

"One of the nurses told me a few minutes ago. It's horrible, but what does that have to do with---oh, I see. Your old anxiety has reared its ugly head, huh?"

"Yes," I said, keeping my voice very low. I wasn't eager to have Jory know how neurotic I am, not since we barely knew each other, not that he probably wasn't figuring it out for himself. And I was pretty ashamed that way too many things scared me way too much.

"Let me prescribe some Xanax. That will help you pull yourself together."

"No drugs." I said. "I hate drugs. Besides I still have some from a year or so ago. I'll be fine." Even as I said it, I was having trouble focusing my eyes. Everything became distorted.

"Well, let's get your head looked at." He pulled out that little thing with a light and looked into my eyes as he also felt around my head.

"You have a bump here," he said. "We need to get an MRI. Will you stay to take her home?" he asked Jory. "It could take an hour or so before we get her in. Or do you want to spend the night here?"

"No. I want to go home." I hated that someone would have to wait around, but there was no way I wanted to spend the night in the hospital. I'd done enough of that at the end of my mother's life.

"I'll take her home." Jory's hand rested on my shoulder. "I don't mind waiting."

"You have to go to work tomorrow and it might be late." I was feeling more and more guilty about being such a baby. I should just spend the night in the hospital.

"Hey, it will give me a chance to catch up on old magazines." He walked over to a table that held at least a dozen magazines, very worn and tattered.

"How are you ladies?" Glen had turned to Mignon and Madge, the former in her constant state of cool and the latter looking more disheveled than ever. Madge's expression said she hadn't missed the quick wink Glen gave Mignon, who pretended to take a tissue from her jacket pocket.

"I still can't believe Horace is gone," Mignon said ignoring the embarrassing, overt flirting in which our medical lothario was engaged. "I wasn't crazy about the stodgy old skinflint, but he was a cousin, and his death will rattle every skeleton out of every Brunson closet. Oh, forget that last part." She looked as if she hadn't realized until then that she was talking to a group of people. "I'm beside myself."

I made a mental note that when my head was pitching and tossing a whole lot less, I would ask her what she meant but the Brunson skeletons.

A nurse walked up announcing that she would take me for my MRI. If I hadn't been in such a state of numbness there was no way they would have been able to get me into that horrifying little doughnut of a thing. As it was, I was in a hazy place where nothing mattered. Before I knew it I was being delivered back to a worried-looking Jory.

"She's fine," Glen said before I had a chance to speak. "She does have a very mild concussion so I don't want her to be alone."

"She can stay with me!" Madge and Mignon announced in unison.

"I just want to go home," I was starting to come back to earth and felt every nerve in my body go on red alert.

"I'll stay with her," Jory said. "I can sleep on the couch. After what happened to Mr. Brunson, I'll feel better watching over her. You ladies are welcome to stay, too. I'll take care of all of you."

I didn't miss the look Madge and Mignon gave Jory, one that suggested he might be taking a bit too much for granted.

"If you're needing someone to look out for you, I'd be more than happy to oblige." Dr. Newell did absolutely nothing to challenge the town's assessment of his being the biggest skirt chaser and horniest widower in town.

"Nonsense," Mignon stomped on his arthritic libido. "I didn't get this far by being a shrinking violet—not that you, E, dear, are a shrinking anything. You need someone to be with you to make sure your head doesn't give you any trouble. Remember, I am not a card-carrying member of the NRA for nothing."

I hated to think that Mignon had guns, but I had heard rumors that in the spring, squirrels were found dead in her yard with bullet holes through their little heads. Mignon hates squirrels, and they sometimes decide to squat on the wrong lawn.

"Well, I want a scotch," Madge rubbed her eyes, causing her mascara to make her look like she was wearing two bull's-eyes. "And I'm thinking of getting a guard dog, something big and fierce. I'm going to Animal Rescue tomorrow."

"You're not serious?" Mignon asked in a tone that said she worried Madge was totally serious.

"Well, if you ladies have no further need of me, I'd better get to Whitey Barnes." Glen twirled his sphygmomanometer around his neck. "Somehow that idiot got a bullet in his rear. I guess Charlie Sutter is tired of Whitey slinking around after his wife when Charley's working nights. But you didn't hear that from me. Of course, in this town, you'll hear it from everyone tomorrow. Good night, my dears." He gave us a courtly bow, but his eyes lingered on Mignon who impatiently waved him off, but blushed nevertheless.

"That man!" Mignon said more aggravated than flattered. "Aren't there drugs to tone down old fools like that?"

"Not Viagra, that's for sure," Madge said. "Duane took it once and it nearly scared us both to death. We couldn't get him to calm down if you know what I mean."

"Oh my god. We know what you mean and can't believe you said it. Come on. We need to go home." Mignon jerked on Madge's jacket hard enough to nearly throw the giant of a woman off kilter.

"Watch it!" Madge pulled her arm away from Mignon's grasp. "You want to put me in the hospital, too?"

"Don't tempt me." Mignon snarled.

Jory returned from making a phone call as the ladies were giving me goodbye kisses and promising to call early the next day. Lucy was with him.

"Aren't you the girl that everyone in town is crazy about!" He said so sweetly that I was glad I had tabled him as a murder suspect. "Are you ready to go home?"

"It was so nice seeing you again." Lucy gave my hand a gentle squeeze. "I hope next time that we meet under more fun circumstances. Jory," she turned to her brother, "I don't work until the afternoon tomorrow. Do you want me to stop and check in on E?"

"I already have that taken care of," he said. "I called Mama. She's going to stop over."

Lucy's face lost her smile. "Mama? Do you think that's a good idea?"

"Of course. Mama raised us. She'll know any signs of trouble. Even though I'm sure E will be just fine." He turned his charm back toward me.

Lucy's concern about her mother's stopping in at my house sent up a red flag. I knew that Jory's father was a gem, but I'd never heard anything about Mrs. Esqueda. That might be a problem because when Camphor can't say something nice about someone, it says nothing at all.

"Oh my gosh," I said as soon as we were in the house and Howler was out in the yard. "I have to call Maurice and tell him I won't be able to finish painting tomorrow—unless you think I could go to work."

"No work." He looked around at the broken pieces of glass everywhere. The intruder took no prisoners. "The good doctor made me promise that you would do very little tomorrow. Now point me toward a broom before you get ready for bed. I have some work to do."

"Here," I handed him the broom and dustpan as I studied the shards of glass that extended from the kitchen to the dining room. "They didn't get the best stuff though," I said. "All my mother's good dishes, glasses and silverware are in the attic, with my dad's papers." I saw pieces of Limoges but it wasn't much, and I knew I was lucky to be alive.

"You'll need to get yourself some new dishes. I don't think whoever it was that did this left many you can use."

His eyes rested on me, creating a burning sensation in all parts sensual and private. Then he went to work sweeping so forcefully that he reaffirmed my gut instinct that Jory Esqueda could take care of anything— and anyone.

Only when I left Jory to go up to my room was I fully aware of the drumbeat in my head. It was followed by an unshakeable sense of danger. I couldn't let Jory see me like this. I practiced even breathing: in, two, three, four, hold, out two, three, four, hold. By the time I heard his footsteps on the stairs, I had calmed down to a seven, with ten being the highest on my panic scale.

"Here is some nice herbal tea." He pulled the comforter that had been my mother's up around my neck. "I'm going to check on you quite a bit through the night."

"Why don't you sleep in the guest room?" I pointed to the room next to mine. "It's fine and that bed is all made up." And I would feel oh so safe and oh so good with you right next to me I wanted to add but didn't.

"That would be far too great a temptation." He briefly touched my cheek. "Besides you have a very comfortable sofa downstairs, and my sleeping there will keep the neighbors from talking."

"As if you and I would be the topic of conversation in a town that has had two murders in less that a week." As I struggled to smile, I felt my eyelids getting very heavy. "There are extra blankets in the--" I was too tired to finish the sentence.

I heard Jory slip in and out of my room several times during the night, but felt only comfort. Nothing could get me when he was around.

Just before I woke, though, I remember a dream laced with grotesque faces and strangers chasing me. I woke at five in the morning, afraid to go back to sleep. I should have taken the Xanax. I'd hesitated because I'd taken it once a few years ago, and it left me feeling more zombie than human.

I lay awake for hours, hearing Jory stirring but not wanting him to see me unwashed with stinky breath. When I did decide to rise, the clock on my dresser said it was after ten o'clock. I panicked remembering that Maurice would have expected me an hour ago. I grabbed a robe and slowly, carefully made my way downstairs to get my iPhone to dial his phone number. Next to my phone was a message from Jory. "I called Mr. Brunson and told him your situation. He said to take all the time you need to heal. Coffee is made. Stay quiet and warm. My mother will be over later, Jory." As a PS, he'd given me his cell number.

What a great guy, too good to be true, really. On that thought, my father's cautionary, "If it looks like it's too good to be true..." ran through my head. Well, my dad wasn't talking about Jory.

I brushed my teeth, put on a pair of jeans, a little looser I was happy to notice and grabbed one of my warmest Michigan sweatshirts. The ladies arrived as I was having my second cup of Jory's surprisingly good coffee.

"Dear," Mignon sipped her coffee and looked at me very seriously, "I didn't say anything last night because we were all in very dire straits. Today, however, I want to remind you that all these houses around us have ears and eyes. It was nice of Mr. Esqueda to volunteer to help out, but this won't do in the long haul. You are, after all, a single woman."

"Jesus H. Christ!" Madge shouted loudly enough to make my head hurt again. "E, I had no idea that Miss Hoity Toity was going to remind you to be moral. You know," she shot her bloodshot eyes at Mignon, "if you'd loosen up and hop in the sack more, you might not be the oldest and meanest spinster in Camphor."

"Well, I never!" Mignon's face was purple with rage.

"That's the trouble—you never." Madge crossed her arms, and retained a very satisfied look.

"Ladies, this is all very unnecessary—and very much none of your business." I was fed up with their meddling—and a little guilty knowing that my mother would have agreed with them. "Jory is just a friend and he has been a big help. Besides, I feel totally safe here."

"We care about you." Mignon looked insulted.

"I know, and I love you, too, but you have to give me credit for some sense."

"We'd like to," Mignon snapped, "but you've just been half scared out of your wits by someone you let barge into your house. And you're dating our gardener's son!"

"Why you snob," I was only half teasing. "And I'm hardly dating him. He's someone I've known for a long time."

"Don't count me in on what she says," Madge backed off. "I don't see one thing wrong with dating a gardener. After all, I married the town junkman."

"Who just happened to be Cissy Brunson Weatherbee's closest living relative." Mignon was fuming.

"Duane wasn't exactly without resources. There's money in junk, you know. Besides, he didn't even know he had a rich relative," Madge got right in Mignon's face. "When we got left that bundle no one was more surprised than we was."

"We were." Mignon corrected.

"You was not surprised," Madge had once again totally misunderstood. "You didn't even know us until we moved in next door to you."

"And what does any of this have to do with what we were talking about?" I was ready to explode. "Never mind; my head hurts. How about if we table this discussion? I'm going to make some herbal tea and go back to bed."

"I'll make the tea," Madge said.

"I'll make it," I said in a very firm, don't f-with me way. "Now you two just go about what you were going to do and I'll be fine."

"But think about what I said about the Esqueda young man, all right?" Mignon cajoled me. "He's not the type you usually date."

"The type I usually date is no type. I haven't had a date in way too long."

"Well, don't get desperate," Mignon said as Madge made a gagging gesture behind her back.

"I won't." No one but Mignon would consider Jory Esqueda a desperation date. "Now how about if you go downtown and see what you can find out about Horace's murder." I gently pushed both of them toward the front door.

"I had better get over to the funeral home and help make plans. Horace's death, old curmudgeon that he was, is going create a mess at Brunson Spice. All of us crazy Brunsons will want a bigger piece of the pie. We are a very greedy lot."

"And stuck up, too," Madge added.

"That's enough." Mignon pushed Madge out the door leaving me in perfect, unadulterated aloneness.

"Howler, you can come out now." Howler appeared from the den, where I knew he'd capitalized on my being held captive by the ladies in order to sleep on the antique velvet chair that had been my mother's prized piece of furniture.

"Is that a velvet thread I see on your rotund self?" I looked at my dog as if he could understand. Honest to god, he looked like he did. "Stay off that chair."

Howler was saved by the bell—the doorbell.

"Junior asked me to stop over."

"Junior?" I still wasn't tracking too swiftly.

"George, Jr." The short woman with gray hair had Jory's beautiful eyes but no smile.

"Oh, you're Jory's mother," I said

"Yes. You must be Elizabeth." She didn't like me. I am used to people either liking me or being able to take or leave me. This woman, who didn't even know me, had a look on her face that said she hated me. Somewhere in the back of my mind, I imagined her singing the West Side Story refrain, "Stick to your own kind."

"Come in." I stepped back to let her pass. She studied my house as if it were riddled with bubonic plague.

"You have a big house." Her disdain was crystal clear, even taking her broken English into consideration. "You need a house this big?"

"It was my parents'." I knew I sounded totally defensive.

"Junior said you are sick, that's why he stayed over. You don't look sick."

"It's a long story," I said. "Anyway, I'm fine. How about if I make you a cup of coffee or tea?"

"No, if there's nothing wrong with you, I'll leave. I have to get groceries and then be home when Selma comes. She's a friend Junior'." Mrs. Esqueda gave me a smile, a sly smile that suggested I needed to know more about Jory and Selma. I didn't care if his mother didn't like me, I now officially hated her.

"Thank you for coming," I waved as she left. Mrs. Esqueda was a huge pain in the keester. What would I tell Jory when he asked me how it had gone with his mother? Now I knew why Lucy had been so upset. And who the hell was Selma?

I plopped down on the sofa. I didn't need any more people stopping in to look after me. It was exhausting. So they were gone, and I should have been able to rest, but alone in my house with my dog snoring on the floor beside me, I let it slowly sink in that two of my neighbors on our very long and majestic street had been sliced up like summer melons. I'm someone who can conjure up a catastrophe with very little help, and now I had major trouble within shouting distance, to say nothing of the break in. I got up and checked both doors to make sure that the deadbolts were on. Then I fell into a fitful sleep.

I awoke with a start as the door opened. "It's me," Jory shouted before he walked in. He'd used the key I had given him to open the door the night before, but he'd scared me nevertheless.

"So you met Mama, huh?" he sat on the arm of the sofa as I focused my eyes.

"Yes, I did. But I don't think your mother is delighted that we're friends. In fact, she seems to think someone named Selma is a much better match."

"I can't believe she pulled that!" Jory nearly fell off the couch laughing. "Selma's family and my family were friends years ago. Then they moved away. When she moved back several months ago, I showed her around town. She's a great lady, but I'm not interested."

"Well, I don't think your mother believes that." I was surprised at how relieved I was that I did.

"I have to go over to Horace Brunson's. His son Taylor called me. He's just arrived to make arrangements for his father's funeral, and he wants the yard looking good because people will be going back to the house after the service Saturday. Want to come with me?"

"I would love to! Let me brush my teeth and comb my hair." My head didn't hurt much, and there was no way I was going to miss seeing Horace Brunson's fabulous place from the inside. I had passed it thousands of times as I walked to and from school or on other errands. It was comprised of several massive stone buildings. His main house and carriage house were rumored to be opulent. For years, Horace hosted lawn parties and Brunson Spice Christmas parties there. I had attended them with my parents when I was little but at that time I was much more interested in Santa and presents than furniture and design. The estate had been in the Brunson family forever and was grand in the grandest sense of the world. It was at the very opposite end of the street, as far away from the Nagel house as you could get.

"You look very good," Jory said when I returned in my new raspberry wool pullover and jeans, "but remember we're going to help set up for a funeral."

"You think I need to put on work clothes?"

"No, you look great. Besides, I was only kidding. You're still recovering, remember?" He looked at me in a way that I couldn't remember anyone ever looking at me. It unnerved me. Maybe he was very, very good at getting what he wanted. Again, I warned myself to watch out.

"Let's go," I broke whatever train of thought he was on and led him out the door.

Cars lined the Brunson driveway reminding me of Mignon's prediction that Brunsons would come out of the woodwork. The door was open so we walked into the elegant foyer, all marble and gold. It housed an assortment of glitz and glamour that I didn't remember ever seeing. The Brunsons were keeping up with the Brunsons. Maurice was in the front room talking with several older men who were similar enough in appearance to him to signal they, too, were Brunsons. I also saw Mignon talking with some well-dressed, stately older women I didn't know. She threw me a quick kiss and mouthed that she would see me later.

"Oh, I'm so glad you came. Look at these bushes." A small, thin, balding man in his forties had begun to shake Jory's hand. "We have to get this place in shape. Father would be furious."

"E, this is Taylor Brunson, Horace's son. Taylor, do you remember the Clarys? E is their daughter."

"Oh, I remember them both very well. And I remember you as a very cute little girl with pigtails and a potty mouth."

"What?" Surely he was remembering someone else.

"No, I remember that you were here for a Christmas party with your parents, and you wanted one of the presents that had been wrapped for another child. Your mother kept gently telling you that you would have to wait. Suddenly you shouted, 'Give me the damn present!' Your mother was very upset."

"Are you sure it was me?" I remembered hearing stories that I had been a very indulged little girl, but here was embarrassingly living proof. "I must have been a real brat."

"I assure you that she is perfect now," Jory edged closer.

"I'm sure she is." Taylor gave me a gracious, practiced smile. Then his attention turned to the needy landscaping. "Do you think you could walk around the yard and see what needs to be done and then try to find time tomorrow to do it? My father hadn't been himself in his last few months or he never would have let the yard get so out of hand. The funeral is Monday. We'd originally set it for Saturday but we had a scheduling conflict. Isn't this whole thing awful?" he asked, as if an afterthought.

"It is." Jory looked meltingly sympathetic. "But as far as the yard, there's no problem. E and I will take a walk around and assess what needs to be done." He waited for Taylor Brunson to return to his guests and then we walked together over the expansive lawn. It was warm for November. We'd been so lucky. No major freeze and a lot of sun. Today was almost more late summer than late fall.

"He doesn't seem too ripped up about his father's death," I said turning back to see the house's elegant and imposing back entrance. "Doesn't it seem like an only child would show more emotion at losing the last of his parents?" I thought back to those first few awful days after my mother's death.

"Grief is a strange thing," Jory said. "You never know in what direction it will take you. And perhaps the apple didn't fall far from the tree. I heard his parents weren't too warm and welcoming."

"Maybe." Taylor Brunson was more a block of ice than a human being. And he certainly was the opposite in build and appearance from his imposing father. I wondered if anyone considered how much he inherited due to his father's untimely and gruesome death.

As Jory made lists regarding what he needed to do, I fought the urge to start rooting through things to see if there were any clues to why Horace died such an unspeakably awful death. Yesterday Horace Brunson had gotten up, dressed, and gone to work just as he had thousands of other days, but this time he didn't return. Sad.

"E, you remember Vi," Mignon glided up with her cousin in tow. I'd only met Violet Brunson Thornton once years ago, but couldn't help noticing that, like Mignon, she never seemed to age. Both women had practically wrinkle-free, alabaster complexions, unblemished by sun and financial strain. Vi was a society granddame in Greenwich, Connecticut.

"You are still very beautiful," Vi said as she took my hands in hers. "Your mother was a beauty, too. Is this your husband?" She turned to Jory with a flirty smile. Violet had been married many times and was known to have had even more lovers than husbands.

"No," I said, "this is Jory Esqueda, my friend." It was awkward, and Jory's lovely mouth formed a half-smile as he watched me try to navigate the waters.

"He's Horace's gardener," Mignon said incredibly rudely. She deserved a spanking—with a huge paddle.

"Oh I wish you lived near me," Vi continued her coquettish behavior. "I have this awful person who doesn't know a pea from a peony. He's a total boob."

"Well, if you lived here, I would take care of all your gardening needs." Jory was thoroughly charming, but I hoped he didn't know that even at her very advanced age, it was more than her garden Vi wanted Jory to tend.

I was so put off by Mignon's bad behavior that I could barely say good-bye to her when she and Vi left. She told me she would call me later, but if she knew what was good for her, she'd wait a few days.

"Well, you are looking very well," Maurice, in a purple cashmere dinner jacket and beige slacks, joined us. "Isn't this the damnedest circus you've ever seen? I don't even know some of these people claiming to be relatives. Won't they be sorry when they hear the reading of the will! Horace was no dummy, and his will is airtight. Taylor will return to run Brunson Spice."

"I was wondering who would live in this wonderful place." I said.

"Now that's still up for debate. Taylor isn't sure he and his wife want a place so Taj. I think there may be some negotiating. All I know is that I don't want this mausoleum." Maurice waved his hands dramatically as he exaggerated the house's nearly imperceptible flaws.

"Any word on who might have killed Mr. Brunson?" Jory asked looking up from his notebook.

"Not yet. They're investigating the possibility of disgruntled workers and even delving into some family squabbles. I guess Mignon had words with Horace before his death. That's what Whitey said this morning anyway."

"Oh, sure," I laughed. "Mignon killed him, right?" The idea was preposterous, but Maurice didn't laugh.

"Well, all I want is for this awful business to be settled." He shot Jory a strange look. I made a note to pump Maurice for all he knew when I was back at work. "See you Tuesday, all right? The funeral will keep me busy Monday so if Tuesday works for you, that's better, E." He gave me one more sweet smile and walked off to join the Camphor four hundred.

"Ready to go?" Jory leaned against me. "I forget that you are still recovering."

"I'm fine," I said, "but it probably is time to get …."

"I'm so glad I bumped into you." Caroline Kidston stood next to her husband. She was, as Mignon would say, "dressed to the nines." "Did John forget to ask you to call me? I was surprised when you didn't."

"I told you that E had an accident," John was uncharacteristically sharp with his wife. "Let's discuss it when we get home."

"Well, I hope you will give me a call. I hear you do a lovely job, and I would like to get the baby's room painted before daddy gets here?" Caroline Kidston was a perfectly dressed, perfectly coiffed bitch.

"Caroline, I have some business to attend to." John was stone as he took his wife's arm and led her out. I heard her say, "You can't tell me what to do," she said as he helped her into her shiny silver BMW.

"That guy still likes you." Jory said when we were both sitting in the *Lawns by Esqueda* van.

"John is old news." I said, hating that Caroline's announcement of having a baby bothered me so much.

"I hope so. I have big plans for us." He brushed my leg as he put the van into gear. "Are you up for a hamburger, a really greasy one?"

Again, Jory's too-familiar way of talking to me left me unsettled, but to my surprise, I was definitely up for a hamburger. My appetite was back and the onion rings, hamburgers and iced cold drinks we picked up at The Little Burger Barn just outside the Camphor city limits were delicious.

"Doesn't this hamburger seem particularly wonderful?" I asked as we sat in the van listening to CDs and eating.

"It's good," he said. "But you're probably also starving to death. When did you last eat?"

"Gosh, I can't remember. But I'll tell you one thing. My head is totally absent from pain. I think I've healed."

"So I don't have to treat you with kid gloves," he said as he ran his hand through my hair. I leaned into it much the way Howler leans into me when I touch places that are particularly pleasurable. "Maybe we could have a cup of coffee at your place?"

"Sure." I said. "I only have regular, though." I couldn't resist, and it both scared and thrilled me.

"I never drink anything else," he whispered in my ear as he put the van into gear.

My hands shook as I got the coffee ready, and for a change it wasn't from panic. It had been a very, very long time since I'd had a man anywhere around who made me feel as alive and aroused as Jory Esqueda, THE Jory Esqueda who made all the girls in ninth grade quiver. Everything was happening too fast, but I'd be damned if I knew how to stop it. I'd blame it on a closed head injury.

"Maybe we could wait on the coffee," he said turning around and kissing me with such sweet force that I melted into him. His kisses were lingering and perfect, masterful. I didn't care if it was the middle of the afternoon and that anyone walking by could see the heat coming from my kitchen.

Then my head stomped on my heart. *What are you doing, Elizabeth Catherine Clary?* "I can't."

"Right." Jory pulled back. "I am usually not so aggressive."

I didn't know that I believed him. "It's not that. I just like to take things slow. And, besides, what would your mama and Selma think?" I tried to lighten the air. "Sorry about the way Mignon treated you. She's from another generation."

"The generation in which girls who live in the biggest houses in town don't date the gardener's son? Truthfully, I can't blame her. She wants you to be with someone special. You deserve that."

His voice was liquid, and his eyes pulled me toward him. I wanted to grab his hand and pull him upstairs, but I didn't.

"Well, I may live in a big house, but I paint people's houses for a living. And I'll throw you a bone. I had the worst crush on you."

"You were too young, but I watched you, you and that Kidston guy who chased after you. Once when I was in the Air Force and all the guys were writing their girls, I thought about writing you a note, but then I thought your mother might go through the roof. Your father had died, but I knew your mother wouldn't want George Esqueda's son writing you."

"What you're saying," I smiled up at him, "is that my mother wouldn't have been any happier than yours was today."

"Point taken." He gently stroked my arm. "But would Catherine Clary have wanted her sixteen-year-old daughter to get letters from the gardener's son?

"Maybe not." I hated to admit it, but I knew that among my mother's many gifts, tolerance was not one. Jory was right. She would not have wanted me to date him. Like most of the town, she'd expected me to finish my master's and marry the genteel, highly-sought-after John Kidston.

Then it came, unbidden and terrifying. "I can't breathe," I pulled away from him and bent over, hoping the blood rushing to my head would help.

"What can I do?" he asked.

The room was spinning and nothing seemed real. Even Jory's voice seemed distant.

"Do you need to go to the hospital?" He held me to him. I could feel my heart pounding against his chest. "Let's go to the hospital."

"No," I calmed down just a fraction. "I know what it is. It's panic."

He continued to hold me gently, soothingly. "Panic? I've scared you? Oh, Elizabeth, I never meant to scare you." He brushed his hand through my hair in calming strokes. My panic went from ten to zero in seconds. "There. Are you better? I know all about panic attacks."

"You have them, too?" I leaned back just far enough away to see his comforting, compassionate face.

"Not exactly. But when I was in Afghanistan, I had friends who had severe ones. I mean why shouldn't they? Some of them had seen their friends maimed or blown up. Others received letters from lovers telling them they were through. It wasn't a good time."

"I can only imagine." My eyes began to focus.

"Why shouldn't you have some anxiety? Look what you've been through. Murder. Break-ins. And this big idiot coming on to you as if you didn't already have a lot on your plate. Let's just rest." He held me in his arms and a zone of safety was created that put me, always on alert, in a state of total relaxation.

We sat next to each other on the couch and though things might be in hideous upheaval on Cinnamon Street, but in my house, two people were comfortable enough with each other to fall sound asleep.

Chapter Five

"E! Are you expecting someone?" I awoke to see Jory straightening the cushions he'd been sleeping on.

"No. Oh, god! I hope it's not the ladies." I practically leapt from the sofa to straighten my hair and clothes.

"Forget the ladies. I hope it's not Mama," he laughed. "How about you open the door? We don't need the whole town to know about this."

"Sure." Jory really did seem to be a dream come true, I thought as I walked to the door. But all good dreams were wiped out when I looked out the window. The person standing there, impatiently walking back and forth was Harvey Barnes, Camphor's chief of police and Whitey's uncle.

"E, I'm sorry to bother you, but I had word that young Esqueda might be here." He tried to poke his head past me to get a look inside the house.

"He is," I said, so much for keeping the relationship under wraps. "I'll get him."

"I'm right here," Jory, pretty well pulled together, joined us in the hallway.

"I don't have time to talk right now," Harvey said very officially, "but I need you to come down to the station and answer some questions tomorrow afternoon." He directed his words to Jory.

"Me?" Jory seemed as confused as I.

"We have word that you were around the Brunson house the night Horace was murdered. I need you to verify your whereabouts."

"I'm sure I was home." Jory looked irritated.

"Not now. We'll discuss it tomorrow. Sorry to bother you, E." Harvey left.

"Shit!" Jory turned to me, "I have no idea what that was about."

"Were you at Horace's the night he was murdered?" I asked.

"E, you don't think I had anything to do with murder?"

"No." I hated that it sounded more like a question than a firm commitment. But after all, what did I know about Jory Esqueda except that he was the hottest guy in the entire universe?

"I'd better go." All warmth and passion were gone. His eyes reflected the anger and hurt that I'd most certainly inflicted upon him. "I'll call you."

"Jory, I didn't mean to sound as though I didn't believe you."

"I'll call you," he grabbed his jacket and left.

I wasn't sure he would ever call again. Worse yet, I wasn't sure I wanted him to. All hell had broken loose in my life in just a few minutes. Why did Harvey think Jory might be involved in Horace's murder, and who had I let into my life and my heart? I needed the ladies. I grabbed Howler's leash, snapped it on, and the two of us headed down the street.

I stopped at Madge's because her house was first, and I didn't think she'd read into me as easily as Mignon.

"Come on in. I was going to call you." Madge held one of the three remaining cats from Cissy Weatherbee's retinue. This one was large, yellow, and went under the deceptive name Lovey. He bit everything and everyone. Madge was the only one safe from his viperous teeth. "I'm worried about Mignon. I think Horace's murder has gotten to her more than she lets on. I've tried to get her to go to dinner, to a movie, anything, but she's so upset, she always says, 'no.'"

"I'm sure she just needs a few days. Mignon's sturdy. She'll bounce back." I knew that it was Madge's incessant yammering, Mignon's words not mine, that were driving Mignon to distraction, but I wasn't going to hurt my wild-haired friend by sharing the information. "Wow! I always forget what a huge house this is." I looked round her totally discombobulated mansion. Newspapers were everywhere and cans of soda occupied every flat surface.

"Duane and I got lost in it the first few weeks we lived here. I can't imagine Cissy living here all by herself. But, hey, I have someone here I want you to meet." She pointed to an enormous object in one end of the room. "This is Hannibal."

For a moment I had no idea what Madge was talking about. Then the enormous object moved. It was a dog—I thought. The head was gigantic and furry, like a lion's, all yellow. The body was short-haired and speckled brown and black. It was the ugliest dog I'd ever seen.

"I told you I was going to get a watchdog." She walked over and gave Hannibal a loving pat. He promptly slid back down and returned to sleep.

"How old is he?" I asked.

"Thirteen." Madge beamed.

"That's a pretty old dog," I said. "You know they don't live to be as old as cats."

"I know. But Hannibal had been at the shelter for two years. If I didn't take him, who would?"

"You're right. Well, Hannibal, welcome to Cinnamon Street." I petted the animal that already seemed to know he was one lucky dog. "Howler and I are going to have to bring you some treats tomorrow."

Howler looked at Madge's newest member of the family and then at me as if to ask, "Is this a joke?"

"Oh I think Hannibal would like treats. Isn't he cute?" Madge said looking lovingly at the lump in the corner.

"He is." I said, thinking that Madge needed to get her eyes checked ASAP.

"Now let's go into the living room. I have some of those wonderful little sodas, in bottles like the old days. Let's have one, ok? Oh and I have chips, too, lots of chips."

"Maybe just a soda," I said, feeling tremendous relief being with Madge. Jory's eyes holding an amalgam of anger and hurt remained stamped in my memory, though.

"Sophie quit," Madge said, offering a partial excuse for the clutter that surrounded her. No loss. Sophie never seemed to be anymore into housekeeping than Madge. "She went to live with her sister in Maine, and, as you know, I've never been Martha Stewart," she laughed.

"It's fine. I was wondering if you know anything about Horace's murder . . . anymore more than we already know."

"Well, Dawn told me that they already have several suspects." Madge's fountain of truth was her hairdresser Dawn Lipschulz, who if not reporting scandal was usually creating it. She was now on her fifth husband, a man in prison for embezzling the funds he used to build her a house out on Lake Camphor. Dawn still lived in it and was divorcing him in order to retain it when his other assets were frozen. She was presently engaged to the lawyer handling the deal.

"Do you know who they're investigating?" I had no intention of telling her about Jory's being a suspect.

"No. Are you all right, sweetie?" She put her arms around me. "You look so sad."

Maybe it was that at that moment she was more my mother than my friend, and maybe I had kept way too much bottled up, anyway, I was soon dissolved in tears and unable to explain why I was feeling so out of control.

"You know what," Madge said wiping tears from her eyes, "we need a pizza from Hot and Spicy," she said referring to our delicious little takeout place that specializes in pizzas and grinders. "I'll order an extra-large one with double cheese and hot, hot Italian sausage. I'm going to have them deliver it. You sit back and rest. I'm leaving for a few minutes to go get us some doughnuts, too. Why don't you call Mignon and have her join us? OK, sweetie?"

"What if Glen's there?"

"Oh, he's not. No car in front."

"And Vi's not here?"

"She left in a private jet hours after she got here a couple of days ago. I wonder if Vi would race out of here before the funeral if she'd been named in the will. Mignon was, you know. Rich as she is, I guess Horace thought she needed more. I hear she's donating it to the symphony and The Camphor Players. Most of Horace's stash went to that nerdy son of his. Must be a disappointment to all those bejeweled Brunsons hoping for more easy money."

"Madge!" For the first time in an hour, I felt like laughing.

"It's true," she insisted. "You should have seen all the worms that came out of the woodwork when Duane inherited Cissy's money. There was people we'd never even heard of. No problem, though, John Kidston and his father were the attorneys and told them that the will was iron clad. Good old John."

"I'll get the doughnuts," I said, not eager to hear Madge again wax eloquent about the wonderfulness of John. "You order the pizza and call Mignon, ok?" I left Howler staring at the comatose Hannibal as I ran home to get my car and drive to Flip's Doughnuts, the best gooey dough balls anywhere. If you get them hot, there's nothing better.

The pizza and doughnuts might be in direct conflict with the greasy burger I'd had earlier, but I was desperate for company. The ladies would be the perfect distraction. Mignon was there when I returned with the doughnuts. Howler was sleeping beside his new best friend Hannibal.

"Oh, E, I'm glad you're here. The craziest thing has happened, and it has me positively apoplectic."

I have never in my life seen Mignon in a state of confusion, but here she was, hair falling from her usually perfect chignon and a button missing on her magenta-colored silk blouse.

"Hey, come sit. What's wrong?" I asked offering both my friends the freshly fried doughnuts that just might hasten all our deaths.

"What's wrong with you?" she asked back. "Your eyes are puffy and red. Are you all right, dear?"

"I'm fine. Tell us what's bothering you."

"Well, if you can believe this, I just got a call from that idiot Harvey Barnes, uncle of the other idiot. Anyway, he wants to interview me at the jail tomorrow. It turns out that I'm a suspect in Horace's murder."

"A suspect! That's crazy." First Jory, now Mignon. Maybe Harvey was rounding up all the unusual suspects in Camphor.

"I can't believe he thinks my best friend would commit murder!" Madge threw her doughnut on a chair and began stomping back and forth across the room.

Then she marched over to Mignon and hugged her so hard that it nearly knocked her over.

"If I ever commit murder, you will be my first victim." Mignon tried to sound angry as she pushed Madge away, but it was clear she was touched by her friend's display of loyalty. "Oh my god! What's that?" she shouted as Hannibal rearranged himself in the corner.

"It's ok. It's Madge's new dog. Let's get back to you." I didn't want Mignon to burst out with something about the dog that would be sure to hurt Madge's feelings, even though it would be one hundred percent true. "Well, no matter how crazy it is to think that you would hurt someone and how sure I am that nothing will come of this, Mignon, I'm calling Earlene. You need to take a lawyer with you. I know that John is your estate attorney, but this calls for someone versed in criminal matters. Can you believe this!" I was now appropriately and completely furious. What was wrong with Harvey that he was accusing a doyenne of the town and one of its most generous citizens?

"We are still having pizza," Madge, always looking for a caloric feast, announced as soon as I'd called Earlene.

"Pizza sounds good. I told Earlene to come here if that's all right."

"Fine." Madge and Mignon said in unison.

I couldn't taste much of the pizza. My mind was whirling with too many thoughts. Front and center was Jory. I still couldn't believe the drug-like effect he had on me. I'd felt so comfortable and secure with him just a short time ago. How could all that have changed so fast?

No matter how much I had on my mind, the wondrous chocolate doughnuts pushed it all aside for a moment. They were delicious. So were the little sodas that Madge is addicted to and always has on hand. In the middle of my second soda, I became determined to call Jory the next day and apologize for ever doubting him. Harvey had made a huge mistake, and I would delight in proving it to him. I would also work a whole lot harder to take it a whole lot slower with Jory, if I got a second chance with him.

Earlene came at seven exactly. She was in a lime green warm-up that announced she was coming from the gym.

"Excuse my outfit," she said as I took her parka. "I was just working out at Slimfest."

"Thanks for coming. I didn't want a rookie to handle this, nuts as it is," I said as I hugged her.

"Girlfriend, I should be thanking you! Do you know my biggest criminal case in the last six months was defending an employee of Jake Herman's who broke into Jake's Bait Shop and stole some of his priciest lures! I'm sorry that Mignon is in trouble but grateful to actually be doing what I was trained to do."

Earlene is half a foot shorter than I am, but she walks with such confidence and power that she is an undeniable force of nature. I was glad I'd called her because I knew her ability to inspire confidence would put the ladies' fears to rest.

Mignon told Earlene what she knew, that she had indeed been to Horace's the morning of his death, but it had only been to assure him she would vote with him to keep Brunson Spice in the family.

"Several people have talked about a takeover," Mignon continued, "but the other major stockholders and I don't want that."

"Well, it sounds as if Harvey is just poking around. I don't think he has anything, but we'll talk to him tomorrow anyway. How about if I pick you up and we can go together?"

"That would be lovely," Mignon was visibly relieved. "I'll wait for you at the front window."

"Wonderful girl," Mignon said as soon as Earlene had left. I didn't think it was the time to remind her about the time I was in high school when she had confronted my mother about my friendship with Earlene, saying that I shouldn't be hanging around with a "black girl." No need to rub anything in. When Earlene graduated as co-salutatorian with me, she made her point.

Instead I said, "I'll meet you there, too." We settled on ten unless Harvey had some other business and I left trying to remember if I had any appointments to reschedule—only one, and I knew I could go to Maurice's early, leave for a bit, and then return to finish.

I left Madge's shortly after Earlene because I wanted to get some sleep and get to Maurice's. If I worked uninterrupted, I could finish the job that day. Then I would have to deal with Caroline Kidston—ugh.

There was no blinking light on the machine so that meant no call from Jory. What was wrong with me?! I had in my clutches a wonderful, perfect man and at the very first test of trust, I let him down. I feared I would not see him or have his smoldering self near me ever again. If I'd had any energy, I would have started crying all over again. Instead Howler and I grabbed chips and dip and ate everything else in the house that was bad for us. Medication by food works for me.

Maurice was up and dressed the next morning. "Do you think we'll finish today?" he asked as he handed me some of Martha's richly roasted coffee. "I am thinking of throwing a little party next week, but certainly don't want to do so if someone clobbers you on the head again or if you don't think we'll have time to get it done."

"I'll probably finish today," I said, "but certainly by tomorrow. I need to be gone from about 9:45 to maybe 11. Is that all right?"

"Sure," he said. "Taylor's having a private, family service Monday. Short and not-so-sweet." Maurice offered. "It's just the most immediate family. I think he doesn't want to run it any closer to Thanksgiving. And I understand that his wife Agnes is none too happy about moving. She likes her life as the wife of a university professor. He'll have his hands full convincing her that we're bliss-filled here in Camphor. But you're not interested in family gossip, and I know you want to get started."

"I understand Harvey already has suspects in Horace's murder." I knew Maurice was eager to attend to other matters, but I wanted to get as much information as possible.

"That's exactly what I hear," Maurice said, always eager to gossip. "I think he's barking up the wrong trees, though. I even hear that Mignon is on his list of suspects—utterly ridiculous. Mignon is one of the few people who didn't find Horace insufferable, two peas in a pod, you know."

"Do you know anyone else?" I kept prodding.

"Not really. The Barneses aren't likely to be up for Genius Grants any time soon, and I don't think they'll be able to do anything until they call in the state police. Well, I'm off to my massage. Hug, hug, kiss, kiss."

As I've said, painting is very good for my anxiety. It wipes all worry from my mind. I rolled that paint on with record speed. It was 9:45 before I knew it. I gave Martha a holler that I was leaving and headed for the jail.

Harvey Barnes looks like Whitey except older. He has one of those expressionless faces that make you wonder what's going on inside—nothing. Whitey and his uncle are devoid of any intellectual curiosity. They're not problem solvers. That's how Mignon ended up a suspect and why the murderer is still on the loose.

"I asked E to be here, too," Earlene said as I walked in and as Harvey opened his mouth to object to my being there.

"I guess it's all right," he grunted.

Harvey's office is small, a few pictures of his now-grown children and a mug presented in 2001 that says, "Best Chief." I'm sure he bought it himself.

"Mignon," he sounded very official, "I've brought you here because there are inconsistencies in your story."

"Oh get off the *Law and Order* jargon," Mignon sniffed dismissively.

"What my client is trying to say," Earlene, all professional-looking and assertive, said, "is that she's not sure what the inconsistencies are and if you have any real reason for her to be here."

"We can't account for her whereabouts," Harvey droned on, still using TV lingo. "Where were you on the night Clara was murdered and the early morning of Horace Brunson's murder?"

"The reason he can't account for my 'whereabouts'," Mignon snarled, "is that I didn't tell him. It's none of his damn business."

I laughed out loud. A little of Madge seemed to have rubbed off on Mignon.

"What my client means," Earlene shot me a look that said no more laughing, "is that she will be glad to detail her activities during those times."

Mignon, too, had been upbraided by Earlene's sternness and got to business letting Harvey know that the night Clara died she'd been shopping and to dinner with Madge and then she went to book club at my house. Then she added, "The morning Horace died, I was with someone."

"Who was it?" Harvey had lost patience.

"I'd rather not say," Mignon said.

"Say!" Harvey ordered.

"No!" Mignon volleyed.

"What will happen if my client doesn't divulge the identity of the person she was with?" Earlene asked, already knowing the answer I was sure.

"She'll have no alibi and will become suspect number one."

"Glen Newell," Mignon shouted. "I was with Glen Newell. Now are you happy, you jackass?"

"One more outburst like that," Harvey said, "and I'll have you arrested."

"No need for that. I think we're done here, isn't that right?" Earlene rose and signaled that Mignon and I do the same.

Harvey nodded and Earlene and I led a very disturbed Mignon out of the building.

"I will see that he is not reelected," Mignon said. "Never have I been so unnecessarily humiliated. And he did it on purpose."

"Why do you think he did it on purpose?" I asked.

"Revenge. A few years back I caught him doing something he shouldn't have and confronted him about it. He's never forgiven me. It cost him his first marriage."

"What did he do?"

"No need for you to find out. It's all water under the bridge. Now, Earlene, let's go get us a huge iced coffee, and I'll write you a big check. You were wonderful. And come with us, E."

I knew Maurice wouldn't mind if I were a few more minutes late so I went to As You Like It with them where I got a gingerbread latte and Mignon kept her promise to write a check so big that Earlene tried to get her to take it back. Mignon refused and told Earlene that she was her lawyer for all future criminal needs. Earlene was a smart little girl, and she'd grown into a smarter big girl and a great friend.

By the time I got back to his house, Maurice was upstairs so I finished the job, left the bill on his table, gathered all my materials, and took one last look. I knew him well enough to know that he would be as happy as I with the results. I also knew it would inspire him to rip down the wallpaper in several other downstairs rooms. More business for E.

As I've said, I'm no cook and knew there was nothing in the fridge so I stopped at the deli to get ambrosia salad and my favorite whipped almond curry chicken salad. Forgive me, dear vet, but I also got some meatballs for Howler who simply adores the deli's barbecued meatballs.

Howler must have been mad at me for leaving him alone all day, because he didn't greet me at the door. Someone else was mad, too, because there was still no blinking light on the answering machine. I put the salads in the refrigerator, poured myself a glass of soda, full of ice, turned on the fire in the fireplace and made myself comfortable in the chair next to it. I sipped my drink and read the Camphor Daily. Not much news, making me even happier with my decision to subscribe to the Chicago Tribune online. I would look at that later.

Well, Howler, you must be mad. I ran upstairs to surprise my dog and command him to get his roly-poly body off my bed. But he surprised me, he wasn't there. I looked in the other rooms. No Howler. Suddenly my mild aggravation was replaced by fear. Where was my dog?

I raced up and down the stairs, looking in all the rooms, under all the beds and even in closets, though I was sure my dog, who was as uncomfortable in tight spots as I, would never be in a closet. Had I left him outside when I went to work?

I looked in the backyard, even inside the decrepit doghouse that my father had made for my old collie Jiggers, but no Howler. Panic flooded me. My eyes couldn't focus, and for a short time I was sure I would die or go crazy. The only thing that kept me from doing either or both was my need to find my dog.

Chapter Six

When I was little, I read Farley Mowat's *The Dog Who Wouldn't Be*, about a man who'd grown up with a crazy and wonderful dog. One day, when he is an adult, the man returns to his boyhood home and finds his cherished pet dead in a ditch. Oh, God, please don't let Howler be dead—or a victim of the Camphor killer.

Clarity returned, and I knew that I had not accidentally left Howler outside. I also knew he had not slipped off by himself to die in a ditch. Someone had taken Howler out of my house and might even have done to him what had been done to Clara and Horace. I spun in circles, panicked about what to do next. I knew of no way to help my dog.

I needed to get someone to help me, but it couldn't be the ladies. They'd be so unnerved that they'd make me warp-speed nervous. And I knew who I most wanted to call, but whether or not he'd answer was a whole other question.

His mother answered the phone. "Mrs. Esqueda, this is Elizabeth Clary," I said. "Is Jory—Junior—there?"

Silence followed by ice. "He is not at home."

"Would you please tell him I called?"

"Yes." She hung up.

The good thing about the coldness with which Jory's mother had answered the phone was that my fear was now coupled with anger, and my regular breathing returned. The panic had subsided. I took a moment to listen, see if maybe Howler was whining somewhere. No little doggie voice. I put on my jacket and walked up and down the street calling his name and listening for a response. Nothing.

I went back home, intending to dial Whitey—though I hated the thought that I would owe him a favor. But a phone call was coming in when I opened the door. I instantly recognized the number.

"E, my mother said you called," Jory's voice was nearly as cold as his mother's but far more welcome.

"Howler's missing. I've combed the house and been up and down the street. I don't know what to do, but you're the person I thought to call for help." I was proud that I was able to maintain my composure.

"I'll be right there." His voice softened. "Stay calm. We'll find him."

I made some coffee, thinking that if I kept busy, I wouldn't be so terrified. I couldn't let my mind wander to what life would be like without my dog nuzzling against me or giving me his special Howler licks. Howler was what was left of my family.

Jory's truck pulled into my driveway before the coffee was finished dripping into the carafe. I was relieved the minute I saw him. The man was no murderer. I didn't care what Harvey and Whitey thought.

"I'm sorry I called you but…"

"It's fine, E, really it is." He put his hand on my shoulder. "Was your house locked?"

"It wasn't. I was late going off to Maurice's, and I must have forgotten."

"E, I'm not going to yell at you, but you know how dangerous it is to leave your house unlocked."

"I know. It might have killed my dog." My voice cracked.

"You didn't kill your dog. We'll find Howler. Where have you looked?"

I told him about searching the house and covering most of the streets in the neighborhood.

"What about your basement?" he asked.

"No. But Howler wouldn't be there. I called his name but he didn't answer. He would have answered."

"Let's look in the basement anyway."

I hate our basement. It's old and the only part of the house that my parents paid no attention to. I reluctantly followed Jory down the creaky stairs to the furnace room. It was embarrassingly dusty. Since the washer and dryer are now in the mudroom next to the kitchen, I seldom go to the basement.

"Well, he's not in this room." Jory said using the flashlight I'd given him to search the hidden spaces.

"Listen." I thought I heard a whimper, a very low whimper. "Jory, I think you might be right that he's here somewhere."

We walked from the furnace room slowly into the totally unfinished backroom, full of dust, cobwebs, and old crates.

"There he is!" Jory flashed his light toward a far corner where a small figure was crouched.

"Howler!" I raced over and embraced his entire body. "Oh, boy, what happened?" His mouth was taped shut, and he was tied by a piece of rope to a pipe. Even once I'd removed the tape and untied him, Howler looked totally dazed and disgraced.

"E, something dropped from the rope." Jory's hand resting on my back gave me strength.

I picked up the paper and could tell it had some writing on it but couldn't read what it said. "Let me borrow your light," I said.

Once I had the flashlight, I read the crudely printed words. "Trouble is very close. Butt out!"

At first I thought I would wuss out and cave to anxiety, but anger followed the panic closely enough to keep me upright. I handed the note to Jory.

"Let's get you and Howler upstairs. Then we'll figure out what this means."

Jory let Howler and me lead and turned out the lights behind us as we went upstairs.

The first thing I did was give my dog a face full of kisses. I could tell that the horrible experience he'd just been through had left him stunned because he didn't even grab greedily for the dog biscuits I fed him. He barely opened his mouth to let me gently place a biscuit one at a time. If I didn't know better, I might think Howler was milking his trauma.

"You have potatoes, eggs, bacon and celery. I'm making us hash browns." Jory came in from the kitchen just long enough to announce what was for dinner and to scratch Howler behind his long, limp ears. "You ok?" His eyes held the kindness and concern that I'd found so magnetic when we first spoke. No way did he kill anyone. I promised myself that I wasn't going to ask him what happened when he talked to the police, and he didn't need to tell me.

"If I'm very good, will you throw in a cold beer?" I asked. Yes, I had a refrigerator full of food, but I wasn't going to give him a chance to leave early. I'd eat the salads another time.

"You have to be very, very good," he said before going to the kitchen. We both knew his meaning was X-rated. "E, in case you start thinking it was very convenient that I was the one who suggested the basement, I have to tell you again that I had nothing to do with the awful stuff going on in this town."

"I know." I rose from the chair, took his wonderful face between my hands, and gave him as deep and meaningful a kiss as I could manage at that moment.

"More to come," he said. "Right now we have other business to attend to."

Even Howler got a plateful of Jory's delicious hash browns. They were good enough to make truckers smile.

"These are wonderful," I said, my mouth full of a blend of crunchy hot potatoes, celery, and cheese. Even the eggs were perfectly done, not runny and cracked and dry like mine the few times I ever tried to make them.

"Good. Are you ready to talk about what happened? About who might have gotten in here and scared Howler to death?"

"It's the second time someone has broken in— though I don't think he had to break in—the more I think about it, the surer I am that I left the door unlocked."

"Any ideas about who it might be?" He leaned across the kitchen table to stroke my arm.

"I know it wasn't you." I blurted it out like some lame middle schooler. "I don't know what got into me, but I know you have nothing to do with the murders. Jory, I'm not usually so dense."

"I overreacted." His hand was tender and warm on my bare skin. "I should have talked it over with you. I was miserable. I barely know you, but I missed you. Crazy, isn't it?"

"Me too. Probably the only person happy about our little fight was your mother." I laughed.

"You know, you're right. She even finagled to have Selma drop over with some tostadas last night. I made an excuse and got out of there fast. I ended up going for a long walk, walked right by here in fact."

"I wish you'd come in."

"Last night probably wasn't the night to visit. It took this guy getting tied to a pipe to reunite us." Howler brushed up against Jory's leg. Even he was not impervious to Jory's charm.

"I'll talk to Harvey about you. I'll make sure you don't stay on the suspects' list."

"No need. I saw him and Whitey this morning. Though they worked pretty hard to convince themselves that I was guilty, turns out I had witnesses to where I was, including a very hot chick on Cinnamon Street—don't worry, I didn't use your name or address. They figured I couldn't have murdered Clara or Horace. People saw me arrive at Clara's, and the time they gave proved to Whitey that I got there after she had been dead for hours. I had been working on Maurice Brunson's lawn at the time. And as for Horace Brunson, though I'd been at his house earlier in the day, people saw me leave, and they also saw me at the barber shop getting my haircut about the time Horace was breathing his last."

I ran my hand through his hair and nuzzled his cheek. "I'm glad. I won't have to visit you in the hoosegow."

"You are stuck with me." He got up, came over to my side of the table and pulled me out of my chair to face him. "You don't mind, do you?"

"You stay right here and keep Howler and me safe."

And that's exactly what he did, all night long, again and again.

Jory was gone when I woke up. All that was left was his woodsy scent on both the pillow and me.

A note posted to the handle of the coffee pot, full of freshly made coffee, said that he would be working all day at Horace Brunson's. He also said that he'd be over after five and that I should keep the doors locked. He ended it with, "Call me if you see a sign of anything suspicious. Yours, Jory."

Mine! Wonderful word. Wonderful man. Wonderful night, so wonderful that for a few hours I'd forgotten the horror of what happened to Howler and the absolute horror of knowing someone was in my house. Though Jory had checked all the windows, doors, and the alarm that I was just getting used to, and had assured me that it was my unlocked door that was probably the culprit, I was scared to death.

Though Jory promised to stop and fill Whitey in on his way to work, I had absolutely no faith in either Whitey or his chief-of-police uncle. How hard is it to find a murderer in Camphor—a town where everyone knows everyone's business? How would I be able to go to sleep at night knowing that the person who murdered Clara and Horace might have been walking in my house?

The panic began with that woozy feeling that always signals it's coming. I've dealt with it long enough to know that it comes unbidden, but strong feelings can ignite it. My feelings were very strong about Jory and the murderer, for different reasons. I knew I had to push forward, to get busy before I was completely overtaken by thoughts of doom and death. I'm not sure Caroline Kidston was the way to escape either of those, but I did have her on my list of to-do's.

And though I'd love to take Jory's advice, stay home and read the new David Rosenfelt mystery on my Kindle, I'd put Caroline off long enough. It was time I faced the music.

"Yes," the voice on the phone was antiseptically uninviting.

"Caroline, it's me, E. I'm sorry it's taken so long, but if you have time this morning or afternoon, I could stop to talk about what you need done."

"Well, finally," she said even less warmly than before. "I was about to call Ed's Painting." Silence.

I didn't tell her how much I wished she would call the slapdash Ed for a paint job that would cost her twice as much as I charge and that would last only a short time before it began to crack and become dull. But I didn't. I was nice.

"Name the time," I said.

"How about noon? I have Pilates earlier and lunch at one with the Garden Council."

"Great." I hung up, not even waiting to hear if she said good-bye. The woman made my skin crawl. John Kidston had to have changed considerably in the last few years, because the man I knew wouldn't look twice such a cold-hearted, backstabbing snob.

With the Caroline Kidston chore settled, I took a shower—stopping to push back the shower curtain every once in a while to make sure I wasn't about to appear in a remake of *Psycho*. Howler, too, seemed to remember the night someone tried to join us because he was already encamped in a corner of the large, old fashioned bathroom.

I threw on work clothes, poured a second cup of coffee to go, promised Howler a walk in the park later in the afternoon, and left. I was careful to make sure all doors were locked. I mentally commanded the panic to go to hell, and since it was a clear, fresh air day, and since the Kidston house on Clovelly was only a fifteen minute walk and I was wearing my Uggs and beige polar fleece jacket, I started walking—sure that the exercise would do me good. I intended to have my free floating anxiety totally under lock and key by the time I met with the anxiety breeding Caroline, who could make coffee nervous .

"E," a shrill voice called down to me, as a pleasant looking young woman ushered me inside. "Audrey will show you to the living room. I'll be right there."

I had just sat down in one of the world's least comfortable chairs when Caroline Kidston glided into the room in a teal blue velvet jacket and slacks which hugged her tall, shapely figure in all the right places. The outfit also made her appear deceptively warm and inviting. I feared that John had not looked much farther than Caroline's alluring outer shell before he proposed. Surely by this time, he regretted his haste. Oh, well, as I'd tried to tell the ladies many times, John Kidston was no longer my business. The fact was, though, he was my friend—a friend I thought seemed to be very unhappy.

"That was my father on the phone. I think I told you he's coming just before Christmas when we spoke earlier. Well, he's also going to be here for Thanksgiving so I hope we can have the renovations fairly underway soon after that. I want this place painted and looking beautiful when he visits over the holidays because it's his present to us."

The house was perfect as it was, if perfect means enormous, showy and no-expense-spared decorated. It was straight out of *Architectural Digest*, but though its outside was Antebellum, for some misguided reason, Caroline had done the inside in glass and angles. To my way of thinking, its exterior was the most beautiful in Camphor, but inside she'd really mucked it up. I recalled Mignon's oft expressed phrase as I looked around, "A lot of class—all of it lower."

"I have some time the first week in December." I reminded myself I was doing it for John.

"Well, I guess that's enough time. I need this room done. I'm tired of this South Hampton yellow." She dropped the name of the most expensive yellow that Overton's mixed. "I want an eggshell, I think. I know you frequently pick out paints for your clients, but if you don't mind, I'll do it. I don't trust anyone but myself. And no offense, but people in Camphor just aren't used to the kind of elegance that I require."

She didn't really say that, did she? What a witch.

"Whatever you think is best. You said there's another room?" I realized that I needed to take a breath because I had stopped breathing when Caroline started talking.

"Oh, yes," a sly smile crept over her face, "we can't forget the baby's room."

"Never." My heart pounded just above my shoulder blades.

"Yes, I think I alluded to it when we met at poor, dear Horace's. The baby is due in April. That's one reason Daddy's coming. He wants to set up a trust at Camphor Savings and Loan. We won't have to worry about college even if baby goes for a medical degree at Johns Hopkins."

"I think she's hiding something," Mignon had said not too long ago when she'd had a particularly bad run in with Caroline. "She acts like she has the world by the tail, but I don't buy it. Something is eating away at her."

Her attitude is eating away at me, I thought, as she went on and on about the baby and the room she wanted to create for him or her.

How ironic that the baby's trust would be at my dad's bank. The bank where my father, the bank's president, was found dead at his desk from a heart attack when I was twelve. John and Caroline were going to have a baby, and they were going to put the money in my dad's bank. Of course I knew I was being irrational. But then again, I am a bit irrational. Dad's bank was the only bank in town, a bank in which I still had a significant investment.

Suddenly it seemed that everyone was moving ahead, into adult living, but me. I hated to admit it, but I realized that somewhere in the back of my mind, John was my fallback guy. If I never found anyone, and if he had the sense to get rid of his hateful wife, then maybe we'd end up two old friends living in houses side by side and recalling the good old days. A baby would change that. John would forever and always have a family that wouldn't include me.

"E, are you all right?" Caroline's smile indicated she hoped I wasn't.

"Oh, sure. I just must have eaten a bad bagel," I said. "Well, how about if you pick out the colors you need and tell Steve Overton? Then we'll be able to get going in a week or so, ok?" I was absolutely perky, and I am not a perky person. I just wanted to get out of there.

"I'm home." John called from the hallway. "Oh, E, I'm glad you're still here."

He looked overjoyed, a fact that didn't seem to go unnoticed by his wife. Predictably, she went all icy. "John, what are you doing here? I told you that I would be busy with E."

"Didn't you want me to sign some papers for your father?"

"You could have done that tonight." Even her cuddly pantsuit couldn't help soften her brittle demeanor.

"Sorry." His eyes went to me. "So, how are you? What's new?"

"Not much." I was uncomfortable with how invisible his wife seemed to him.

"E and I were talking about the baby." Caroline raced through her words.

"Oh I'm sorry. I'm sure our baby is of little interest to anyone but us." He looked at me with those empathy-filled eyes that understood everything you told him and that returned understanding and compassion. John had gotten me through my first panic attack. We were seniors in high school—a stipulation he'd insisted upon when his parents sent him away to school. He'd go but wanted to return to Camphor for high school. Anyway, I'd just been told I had to make the salutatory speech—he was valedictorian. Like many people, public speaking is my number one fear, but unlike most of those people, I zoned out—absolutely zoned out when the principal gave me the "good" news. John had been there when the shakes and blurriness attacked. He got me out of the principal's office and into the fresh air, where my breathing resumed a normal pace.

"You're sorry!" Caroline was screeching at her husband. "You're sorry!"

"I didn't mean that." John went from warmth to indifference. "I meant that I wanted to give E the good news. We are, after all, old friends." He was as uncomfortable with his wife's outburst as I was.

"Well, wouldn't it be nice if E were the baby's mother!" she was still screeching.

"Leave!" John commanded her. "I'll talk to you in a minute."

John was apologizing to me as his wife went upstairs alternately sobbing and shouting swear words that would make even Madge blush.

"She's emotional right now."

"It's fine. She has a lot on her mind." I found myself in the uncomfortable position of apologizing for Caroline Kidston, a woman I couldn't stand. It was pretty obvious that her husband couldn't either. "You'll be a great father, John." I touched his arm, but withdrew my hand quickly fearing his wife might race down the stairs wielding a knife. "I'd better go."

"Are you still dating that Esqueda character?" He asked as he walked me to the door. "He's just no good for you."

"John, I think you better let me decide who's good for me."

"E," he lowered his voice and stepped toward me. I backed away.

"We had this talk a while ago," I said. "You'd better go upstairs and see if you can help your wife."

As I frequently do when I'm in dire straits, I got through the moment and then collapsed. My legs turned into blocks of wood and my arms fell dead at my sides. When emotions collide, panic is sure to rear its ugly head. For a minute I was sure I wouldn't be able to make it to my car and then home—to safety. I couldn't go back and ask John for help. If I hadn't been totally sure that the days I could lean on him for support were over, I was now. I didn't know what would happen in his and Caroline's awful marriage, but I didn't want to be part of whatever they did. John was trapped. And so was Caroline.

I walked down Clovelly taking a last look at Kidstons' gargantuan structure and thinking that house and home are two such different words. Then I headed toward As You Like It to get to a mocha latte before I joined Howler to return some phone calls and do some accounting. I'd been negligent in my business—One Lady Painting—bookkeeping ever since the first murder.

I didn't get to the coffee shop. There were tons of police cars at the police station. There were cars from Dowagiac and also state police cars. Right next to the yellow crime tape were two figures I knew oh too well.

"What are you doing here and what's going on?' I asked Madge and Mignon who never took their eyes off the door of the police station.

"Madge heard about it on her scanner." Mignon said proudly as if Madge was her snitch. "She called me."

"About what?" I asked, sure that I didn't want the answer.

"Harvey Barnes was found stabbed to death early this morning."

"Harvey? Our police chief Harvey?" I felt the panic begin.

"Our Harvey," Madge said wiping tears away, forgetting that she had never had a good word to say about Harvey since he'd ticketed her for going fifty in a fifteen mph limit. "Dirty flatfoot," had been the way she'd referred to her now much-cherished Harvey.

"This is totally out of control." Mignon said. "Someone needs to do something."

That someone wasn't going to be me. I felt dizzy and weak and became terrified that I would pass out, thereby scaring the ladies to death. The thought that I might be the cause of either of their deaths made me even dizzier.

"I'm going home." I said hoping I had the strength to walk.

"Don't you want to see the corpse?" Madge's eyes remained fixed on the doorway.

"I'll pass," I said, hoping I didn't pass out.

"Fine, dear. We'll have tea later." Mignon too was riveted to the place where any minute a stretcher might bear of the body of our reliably incompetent police chief. Poor Whitey. He'd be stuck with finding his uncle's murderer. Poor Camphor.

With one foot in front of the other and shoving every horrible thought that threatened to attack out of my mind, I got home. Panic started to win as I searched for my keys to open the door. My hands shook I was so terrified I might not get inside to safety.

I found them and nearly fell inside the door, feeling silly and stupid. Why couldn't I be like a regular woman and get a migraine when I got anxious? Not me. I had to have a meltdown worse than Frosty's.

Howler was right there to greet me. Immediately I began to reconnect to reality.

"Another murder, guy."

Howler's look was quizzical, asking, "Are you telling me something bad, or are you telling me I can have a dog biscuit?"

I gave him the dog biscuit and then reconstructed that last few hours' events. Caroline and John Kidston were the couple from hell and about to become Mommy and Daddy. Harvey Barnes, an object of irritation and derision for as long as I could remember but a Camphorite nevertheless, was dead. Three murders in just over a week and no end in sight.

Clara, Horace, and Harvey. Not one thread of evidence toward solving their murders.

When I pushed the button on the answering machine, it announced that I had two messages. The first was welcome relief.

"E, this is Jory. I just heard that Harvey Barnes is dead. Lock your doors, pour a soda, and don't move until I get there, which will be within the next hour.

The second message was garbled. I thought the machine had gone bad, but when I replayed it, I knew the problem wasn't the machine.

"Do you think three need company?" The voice asked through the scrambler. "Keep out of other people's business, or the girl they adore will be number four."

All that work to breathe evenly and put one foot firmly in front of the other to get home didn't matter now. The voice on the phone sent me face first to the floor, my head barely missing the telephone stand on the way down.

The pounding at the door roused me. I must have fallen like one of those ladies in a Victorian novel, very slowly and gracefully, because nothing hurt except my ears from the excessive pounding.

"Why didn't you answer?" Jory stood accusingly in the doorway.

"Long story," I said. I didn't want another run to the hospital where Glen Newell would push me to take chill pills, and everyone would stand staring, waiting for me to explode or implode. "Come in and sit down."

"So Harvey Barnes is dead, very dead."

"It's like we're living a nightmare." I put my hands over my eyes. "This is a small town. If someone doesn't do something quickly, we could cease to exist."

Jory's protective arm encircled me. "Well, the good news is that help is on the way. My brother-in-law Javier will be working the case along with his buddies at The State Police."

"It's about time. We have only one police officer left. One day I'm living in this perfect small town where everyone knows and trusts everyone else. Now we look at each other as if one of us could be the killer."

"It wasn't too long ago that you were looking at me that way."

"No more." I couldn't look at him. "But someone is a really bad guy and no one is able to catch him."

"Mama wonders if you want to come for Thanksgiving," Jory did an amazingly good job of going from bad to worse.

"Who's cooking? Selma?" I kissed his neck and ran my hands over his enviable six pack.

"Oh, she's going to be there. No offense, but when I asked why she'd invited Selma, she said I could invite you, too."

"If you don't mind," I kissed his mouth slowly as I got the words out, "I'll take a rain check. Though I haven't bought one thing for dinner, I think I'm cooking for the ladies. I was going to invite you, but sounds like you'll be busy."

"To keep Mama from blowing a gasket," he said. "But if you invite me, I'll come for dessert."

"Don't feel free to bring Selma." I pretended to joke, but I wasn't thrilled that Selma was still in the picture. Jory and I weren't secure enough that I felt comfortable with another woman hovering nearby.

"Selma is not important," he kissed me again, assuring me for that moment that I was the only woman in his life.

Jory wasn't gone ten minutes before Madge called.

"E, can you get down here? I'm so upset. Please."

I raced down, forgetting my Uggs and sliding every inch of the way in my tennis shoes. I rang the bell at the same time Madge opened the door.

"Look," she pointed. "He's just leaving. He's been there every night for the past five days."

A vintage Buick LeSabre was parked in front of Mignon's. I immediately recognized it as Glen Newell's.

"Madge, I thought something was terribly wrong— that you were standing with the murderer poised to slit your throat."

"Don't be ridiculous. I'm worried about Mignon. Suddenly, she doesn't care about her reputation. That Romeo has been there for hours. I don't think they've come up for air." Madge grabbed her binoculars and went to the window of her unbelievably cluttered living room.

"Don't look into her house," I tried to grab the binoculars.

"We're her only friends. We have to save her."

"It's not like she's with Jack the Ripper. And besides, he just left." I took Madge by the shoulders.

"It's not like she can't have an occasional fling. The woman's not dead," I added.

"Glen Newell is a dog. There's no one he hasn't slept with." She said. "Except me. He hasn't slept with me."

"Well, it's not our business. Let's you and me go get a sandwich. I'm hungry."

"It's late. We should stay here." She still had the binoculars pointed at Mignon's.

"Madge, you are going to get Mignon really mad. Let's go get a burger."

"Ok. I am hungry." She handed Hannibal a dog biscuit. He rose slowly, took it, and then lay down and went back to sleep. "And you can tell me all about your love life. I noticed that Esqueda kid was at your house again."

"His name is Jory, and I think you need to get your own boyfriend and leave Mignon and me alone."

"Duane was it for me," she said, her eyes watering as they always did when she mentioned her late husband. "Oh, once in a while an old friend stops by but that's just sex."

"Madge, I don't want to hear it." And I didn't. Madge's men were always twenty years younger and interested more in her money than her body. She knew that, and the surprise was that she was using them more than they used her. I imagined that these last ten years had made her boy-toys more escorts than lovers. We never discussed it, though, and I didn't intend to start now.

We took Madge's car. "I hate this little thing," she said of her Mazda. One of her "friends" had sold it to her. She looked too large for it. She should have Mignon's big Lincoln and Mignon should have this car, I thought.

The Burger Barn has great food, surprisingly good for Camphor which, besides The Fireside, has no great cuisine. The rest of the diners are mostly dives known for grilled cheese and tuna sandwiches. Even the tuna sandwich is terrific at The Burger Barn, grilled on thick, chewy toast and containing a mixture of pickle relish, mayonnaise and other ingredients that I've never identified or been able to duplicate.

"This was a very good idea," Madge slid into the booth opposite me. "I'm going to have Captain John's Buster Burger. I haven't had that in so long. And I'm going to have a humungous soda, too, even if the caffeine in it will keep me awake most of the night. Who can sleep anyway?"

"Great. I feel like a BLT, on their luscious oatmeal bread. And I'm going to splurge and get a green river float. This is my treat so have whatever you want."

"Well, ok. But before we order," she said, "I want to tell you something."

Given the goings on in Camphor lately, I braced myself.

"You know your mother was like a sister to me," Madge was very serious, "and that you are like a daughter. Well, since this past couple of weeks has shown us all that life doesn't go on forever, I want you to know I went to John Kidston's office last week and named you the main beneficiary in my will. Now, it's not all sugar. You'll have to give Hannibal a home."

"Oh, Madge," the words caught in my throat, "I know you love me. You don't have to do this. Really, I have plenty of money, and I know that Duane has nieces and nephews. Shouldn't you consider them?" I didn't touch on Hannibal because of course I would take him, but I doubted he'd outlive his mistress.

"I know, but the only thing Mignon and I have ever agreed on is how much we love you. She went with me and did the same thing. She asked me to tell you, though. She doesn't want to make a big thing of it. Just let her do it. The Brunsons don't need her to leave them any more money."

"And about Duane's relatives. I left them something. And I've done plenty for them these past few years. I'm a rich woman, you know," she smiled. "But we wasn't that close to them. Most of them didn't even make it to Duane's funeral. You're a very special girl, and I love you like a daughter."

"And I love you." I squeezed her hand and felt enormous guilt for every angry thought I'd had regarding her and Mignon. "And you are very, very, very special. Besides, you are also going to live for a hundred years so no more talk of this."

"I just wanted you to know. John said I should tell you. He's made sure you won't hear from any shirttail relatives. It's a tight will—that's his specialty. He will give you a copy of the will."

My mind returned to John and how sad I felt watching him try to deal with Caroline earlier. Maybe my feelings for him ran deeper than I'd thought.

As Madge gave the waitress her order, I looked across the aisle and thought one of the two men sitting opposite us looked familiar.

He rose and walked toward our table. For a minute, I was a bit nervous. "You're E, aren't you? I'm Jory's brother-in-law Javier Rodriguez." Javier was shorter than Jory but stocky and handsome in a dark, swarthy way.

"It's nice to meet you. What are you doing in our little burg?" I didn't know if I should reveal what Jory had told me about Javier's being in on the investigation.

"You guys have been having a lot of excitement lately. A few of us," he gestured toward the man he'd left in the booth, "are helping with the investigation."

"The murders, you mean?" Madge's eyes had left the menu and were now fixed on Javier.

"Oh, I'm sorry, Javier. This is my good friend, Madge Bobik. Madge, this is Jory's brother-in-law. He's in the state police."

"Thank Jesus H. Christ," Madge shouted out. "We have been dropping like flies here. People are getting slaughtered, and the idiots around here don't have any idea what to do."

"I think Madge may be painting perhaps too grim a picture." I felt my breathing start to speed up.

"You know, I think she's right. In fact, I don't you think you ladies should be out much later. And check your houses when you get home, ok?"

There was no escaping it. After Javier returned to his colleague, I recognized that I might want to run, run, run from the truth of what was going on in Camphor, but I couldn't. We had had three murders and no one seemed to be able to collar the killer.

"This is good," Madge ate her giant-sized burger with gusto. I could barely manage a few bites of my sandwich. "Let's go out past Brunson Spice before we go home," she said.

"You know," I said, "that is probably one of the worst ideas you've ever had. Didn't you hear Javier say that we should go home?"

"Please," Mignon said. "I don't want to go inside the building or anything, but I have this feeling that somehow Brunson Spice is connected to all this. Two of the people were connected to the company. Maybe driving out there will give us an idea of something the police have missed."

"But one of them, Harvey, was our sheriff. How was he connected to Brunson?"

"That's what we need to figure out. E, we have to get some answers because it's been weeks, and almost every week another person dies."

"But come on, Madge, do you think the two of us can do anything? "

"We can sure as hell do more than we've done, right? Duane would be saying to me, 'Come on, Maggie, get some balls.'"

Madge is a wheedler and she wheedled me into promising her that we'd take a slow drive past Brunson Spice on the way home. I knew it was a bad idea from the start.

Just how bad I was yet to find out.

Chapter Seven

Brunson Spice is a Fortune 500 company that runs nearly the length of Camphor. Its dozens of buildings are as long as our downtown and run parallel to it. In the dark, it looked like an incredibly long ominous, freighter. Though each building was lighted, the lighting seemed dim and dangerous.

"Well, it's certainly huge, and it's put Camphor on the map," I said as Madge parked the car and I considered the riches that the Brunson family brought to our town. "Any ideas?" I asked after we'd both studied it for about five minutes.

"Let's go by the main building," Madge was not hearing anything I was saying.

"Why?" I asked as she started to drive very slowly toward the building.

"E, we're here and we need to be brave!" Madge opened her door as soon as she put the car in park and pulled out the key.

"Madge! Get back in the car," I shouted. "Don't!"

She was out of the car and headed toward the administration building. Maybe she thought that she'd lived a good long life, but my knees were bumping together to remind me that I still had a long life ahead of me. For a second, I considered letting her go off in the darkness alone, but only for a second. Wherever she was, my mother would never forgive me for letting one of her oldest and dearest friends get her head blown off, or worse.

"Wait for me!" I shouted hurrying, against all my better judgment, after her.

"Spooky, huh?" Madge was having a ball. Her eyes radiated the rush of excitement she was experiencing. Even in the dim lighting, I could see she was fueled by what was terrifying me.

"What on earth are you thinking?" I sounded like my mother the day she found me cutting my hair when I was six. I had wanted bangs, but quickly learned that you don't get them by lifting the all the hair at the front of your head and cutting it to within an inch of your scalp.

"In my gut, I am certain that somehow Brunson Spice is connected to all the terrible stuff going on in this town," she whispered as we stood at a side window of the main building. "We need to get in there."

"Do I need to get you a doctor?" I whispered back. "Are you having some kind of mental breakdown?"

"It's open." Madge lifted the window through which we'd been staring. Before I could stop her, she successfully aimed her considerable heft and struggled through the opening.

"Come on in," she whispered and gestured from inside.

I didn't know how Madge had managed to get her osteoporotic self inside, but I sure as hell wasn't going to be outdone by a senior citizen. I jumped through the window, jamming my knee against the sill.

"You realize that if we get caught, we get arrested." I rubbed my aching knee.

In truth, there was no problem. Madge and Duane were left a bunch of Brunson stock by his Aunt Cissy. My parents, too, had a significant amount of Brunson stock in the portfolio I inherited. And Madge was right, there was no way that Mignon would let us rot behind bars. Nor would John.

I didn't have the heart to tell her that I was sure that Mignon would spring me right away, but she might derive so much delight in seeing her nosy friend in jail that she might decide to leave her there overnight.

The room we were in was large, but sparsely furnished and had that musty smell reserved for very old houses and people. I'd heard many times that Horace Brunson, for all his billions, was a tightwad.

Nevertheless, signs of the spice company were everywhere. Empty jars with various Brunson spice labels were scattered on a table and a desk. There were also brochures advertising the world-renown company.

"We need to get out of here," I said to Madge who was trying to force open a drawer in the antiquated, bottle-strewn desk. The only light we had was the penlight attached to her keys.

I tried to remember to keep my breathing even. My head, though, was ready to burst from the tension of keeping quiet and moving stealthily so no one would know we were where we shouldn't be.

"E, we're here. I think this is Horace's office. In fact, I'm sure it is. I've been here a couple of times. I remember the smell—cigars and money. We need to look around. I bet we find something in here that gives us a clue to what's been going on."

As Madge became more emboldened, I became more certain that being there was the dumbest idea she'd ever come up with. "I don't care whose office it is. We need to . . . I began," and then I heard the sound which I hoped against hope was a routine settling of the old building but feared deep down that it wasn't. Footsteps rapidly headed in our direction. I pushed Madge down behind the giant desk before I hid behind a shabby leather chair in a corner and prayed that the steps would continue right on past the office we were in. The room was beginning to slowly spin. Another minute or two and I would be in real trouble.

"Psst." Madge leaned out from behind the desk. "Who do you think it is?"

"Shhhh." In her wild craziness to solve the murders, Madge forgot we could end up in jail for breaking and entering. No footsteps. Maybe the person had passed by.

Then the doorknob turned, and the room suddenly had a dozen bright lights. My eyes struggled to adjust to the change in lighting, and my heart ka-thump, ka-thump, ka-thumped in my ears.

"E! What the hell are you doing here?" John Kidston was beyond furious. "And , Mrs. Bobik! You brought Mrs. Bobik! Have you lost what little sense you have left!"

"Actually," stammered Madge, "I brought her."

I barely heard the rest of the exchange for two reasons. The first was that I experienced a blissful, totally thankful relief that it was only John who entered. The second was that I was stung by the way John talked to me. He'd never in all the time I'd known him spoken so harshly to me nor had he spoken with so little respect.

Inside me, an explosive anger replaced a possible panic. I didn't care how wrong it was for Madge and me to be there or how ridiculous we must have looked to him crouching behind furniture like trapped animals. "Well, what are you doing here?" I shot back for no rational reason. He was, after all, the Brunson lawyer and had a right to be there. We, on the other hand, would have a hard time getting anyone to believe we had any right at all to be crouching behind and under furniture late at night.

"Not that I have to tell you," he said, flashing a snarkier side of him than I'd ever seen, "but I will say that I've been doing a little digging for Brunson, and we've just discovered some of Horace's private papers are missing."

"What papers?" Madge jumped from behind the chair to stand so close to John they might have been conjoined twins. "Do you think the missing papers have something to do with the murders?"

"E, I'm disappointed in you." John's tone softened barely. "I got a call that someone thought they saw movement in here. Whitey was at the funeral home or he would have found you here. Believe me, he would have been a lot rougher on you than I'm being. You can't do things like this with a murderer on the loose, you know." Only then did Gentle John return.

"Sorry." I was again ten with my hand caught in the cookie jar. "We'll leave right now."

"And don't come back." The unfamiliar sternness returned. "You could have been killed." He took my arm in a way that was both intimate and unnerving. Maybe old feelings and emotions never really totally disappear. It was a thought I decided not to investigate any further.

"Ok." I said stepping back so that he would have to release me. "We'll go home now."

"And stay there. I don't want you to be the next victim." He turned from me to guide Madge out the door.

"Well, are you proud of yourself?" I snapped at Madge as soon as John went back inside. I was mad, embarrassed, and frightened. What was I thinking following goofy Madge into a building and inviting someone to catch us—or kill us?

"Yes, I am happy," Madge wasn't about to admit she might have made a gross error in judgment. "We learned something new, and that's just what I set out to do. Now we're closer to solving the murders."

I cringed at her words. "We are not solving anything, and all we learned is that some papers are missing." But what I didn't tell Madge was that I, too, was getting the fever. I wanted to know who had committed the murders, and I feared that those doing the investigating weren't making much progress. I agreed with Madge more than I felt safe letting her know.

"Don't you think it's strange that them—those—papers are missing just when the whole town's getting chopped up?"

Madge had become either America's version of Miss Marple or a creaky Nancy Drew. I was becoming fed up. "Madge, we need to do what John said: get home and stay safe. We are not policemen," I reminded her as I opened the driver's side door to let her in.

"And that's a very good thing," Madge said. "The police haven't been one bit of help. Oh, but let's not tell Mignon what we've been up to tonight, all right? She has her little secrets. Now we have ours."

Ah ha! The evening spent in sleuthing made more sense. It was to top Mignon—and topping each other was regular sport for Madge and Mignon. Our foray into danger had been to give Madge bragging rights that Mignon didn't have. I had been beyond stupid to go along. But I did agree that we had learned something: papers were missing. That might not seem like much, but it was more than we'd had before. I had also learned that John Kidston harbored anger toward me that erupted in odd ways. And I had to admit that his disappointment in me had a surprisingly painful effect. Maybe my mother's death had caused me to shut down feelings I should have examined. Those feelings threatened to complicate my life in ways I didn't have the time or courage to contemplate at that moment.

Madge was quiet on the drive home until we drove down Cinnamon Street. "Disgusting!" Madge said as we saw Glen Newell's big sedan still parked in front of Mignon's house. "At least it isn't that ridiculous little sports car of his. The man is too old and too stupid to live."

"Let's not talk like that," I urged her, "considering how things are going in town right now."

When we got inside Madge's, I turned on the lights and walked all through her house to make sure she was safe.

"Where's your fearless watchdog?" I asked.

"In his bedroom. I made a bed for him in the guest room, a big doggie bed, and he loves it so much. He goes to sleep fairly early, and then I give him his breakfast in bed."

"I thought he was supposed to guard you."

"Oh, if someone came after me, he'd rip their head off. I just know he would. He is so loyal and so smart. You should see how quickly he caught onto the doggie door I put in. All I had to do was crawl through it a time or two myself, and he totally got it."

"I'll bet he did." I was afraid I'd crack a rib stifling my laughter. "Now keep your doors locked, and if anything at all scares you hit the police on your speed dial. Do you remember? Number one gets you the police."

"Yes, but a lot of good they'd do. Hannibal has everything well in control."

I had no answer for that so I hugged her goodbye and left.

I also thoroughly checked my own house. The way Howler, who'd been more nervous than usual since his ordeal, sauntered in to greet me, I knew that we'd had no intruders. The answering machine light blinked, but I didn't check to see who it was. If it was Jory, he'd call again, and if it was someone bent on scaring me into catatonia, I didn't need to hear it. Besides if I did still have feelings for John, how would that impact what I felt for Jory? I was too tired to think about it. And what if I did still have strong feelings for John, what difference did it make with Caroline Kidston smack in the middle of John's life? No matter how unpleasant she was, she was his wife.

I made a cup of hot chocolate and grabbed a couple of my mother's cookbooks. Thinking about Thanksgiving was better than considering who the next victim might me. In my case, it was the fresh turkey I'd reserved at the market. I knew exactly what recipes I wanted and began the search. My mother was a good but not highly innovative cook. She made the same Thanksgiving meal until our last Thanksgiving when she was so riddled with cancer that Mignon, Madge, and I scrounged the recipes so we could give her the Thanksgiving she'd so often given us.

I never issued a formal Thanksgiving invitation to the ladies. It was understood that when they were in town, we'd be together. Since my mother's death, they spent most Thanksgivings and Christmases with me. Madge always came to my house for the holidays and with the rare exception of visiting a relative somewhere in the world, Mignon was there, too. More and more, though, she hated to fly at the holidays so I had a feeling that this year Mignon wouldn't want to stray too far from home. I intended to make a ton of food so we'd all have leftovers. And Jory would be there for dessert, a very late, very seductive dessert.

My mother's vintage Betty Crocker cookbook had most of the recipes I wanted. I wrote down the ingredients for turkey dressing, giblet gravy, and apple pie. I knew that the Libby's can had her pumpkin pie recipe on it, and that her make-ahead mashed potatoes and cherry salad were in the Camphor Cooks cookbook by Sue Marvin, a celebrated local cook. Madge would bring her candied sweet potatoes, and I'd asked Mignon to bring dinner rolls. To my knowledge, she never did more than open a can of soup, even during the brief marriage she never talked about. I would keep the meal simple and have a great coffee and some interesting wines. The ladies never turned down good wine.

But I had more to think about than Thanksgiving. The first murder had occurred weeks ago and still not one suspect had been identified. If the police suspected someone, they were keeping it under their belts. All the rest of us could do was wait like sitting ducks, hoping we weren't the Camphor butcher's next victim. I hated it. Part of me wanted to climb into bed and stay there until the murders were solved. And the other part of me was itching to get in there and help solve them. Clara had been dead for weeks and was nearly forgotten after Horace Brunson's death. She had become as anonymous in death as she had been in life.

Oh and then there was the rotten job I had to do right after Thanksgiving. What fun it wouldn't be to paint Carolyn Kidston's baby's room. A river of dread pulsed through me when I thought about it. I wished John had encouraged his wife to employ any painter but me. Besides the obvious conflict of interest regarding her husband and me, Caroline was rumored to be the worst person to work for since Sweeney Todd. And when I considered how nasty John had been when he caught Madge and me at Brunson Spice, I was doubly mad at myself for taking the job. I didn't feel like doing him any favors right then.

Once I finished marking recipes and making the grocery list, I caught up on my email. "Dear Suzi," my note began to my college roommate. "I have had a couple of calls from you, but things here have been busy." I went on to tell her about the Camphor murders, but glossed over them so that she wouldn't be so worried that she'd show up on my doorstep. I didn't need to worry her, and there wasn't one thing she could do anyway, except spirit me off to Chicago to stay with her. Spending time in Chicago with Suzi is always fun. Spending those same days with Suzi and her controlling, know-it-all husband is far less fun.

"Are you there?" The IM came through as I was finishing my e-mail. "Wasn't such a great idea to go snooping at Brunson." Pain shot from my fingers to my elbows. "Maybe you and your meddling old goats have lived long enough."

"Stop this! Stop this!" I e-mailed back before I slammed the computer shut. The person had referred to Madge and Mignon as "old goats." My God! It was someone from town—maybe someone right next door. I couldn't breathe; I couldn't move. It was late. I was alone. If I died from panic, no one would find me until morning. I began to rise, but my legs wouldn't do what my brain told them to do. My chest ached, and my eyes didn't focus. Maybe it was the concussion. Maybe the damage had been more severe than I thought. Maybe it was a heart attack. People my age have them. They're the silent killer. *E,* I told myself, *get over this. Your worst fear is fear. That's what will kill you. You need to do something about the person who is stalking and plaguing you. Use your head. Get mad and get moving.* It took only a few seconds for me to know that I wasn't going to die or go crazy.

I looked toward the couch where my dog was staring at me, asking what was going on with me. He was also where he was not allowed to be. "Howler, get off." My dog reluctantly jumped from the couch. I knew he wasn't the one I should be yelling at. I walked over and petted his head. "You are my only buddy tonight. You'll guard me won't you?"

My first inclination was to call someone, either Jory or the police, but I wasn't going to run to either one. It was late, and if I became as frightened as my evil emailer hoped, he would win. I was going to handle it myself.

I looked around the room. The house was deadly silent, and the windows seemed far too open to prying eyes. I quickly drew the curtains. Then I went from the family room to the living room to pull those curtains shut, too. My head still spun a bit, and I was still sick to my stomach. But I was taking care of business. I was glad I hadn't called the ladies because if they knew how the murderer referred to them, they would have been driving all over town hunting him down. I knew they both had massive security systems and hoped they had set their alarms. I wished I'd set Madge's before I left. Hopefully, Glen Newell would offer some protection for Mignon, but what that would be I couldn't imagine.

Truthfully, I was scared but I was also tired of running to Jory, someone I barely knew. No matter how great his physical and emotional appeal, he still was someone very new to my life, and though I hated myself for saying it, he was still someone I couldn't let myself fully trust, partly because he was a man and partly because his story still didn't totally add up. Why was he everywhere that murders happened? I forced my mind to stop spinning.

As I prepared for bed, the phone rang. It took all the courage I had to answer it. "E, this is John."

"Hello." I was still angry at the snotty way he'd treated me at Brunson Spice.

"I'm hoping I can stop by tomorrow," he said. "There are some questions about the papers that are missing, and I'm hoping that your father's files might have some answers."

"John, I wouldn't know where to begin."

"Let me take a look, ok? I'll have Javier Rodriguez with me. We can't figure out why certain files are no longer there."

"Ok. I'm going to make a run to the grocery store in the morning. How about you come by after one o'clock? And let your wife know, ok? I don't need her angry with me."

"I'll handle Caroline," he said. "And, E, I'm so sorry about what happened at Brunson the other night. You know I would never hurt you, right?"

"I do." I hung up. There was no way I wanted to hear those words from him, those words I'd heard when I was twenty-four and my mother had died weeks before. John was there, always there to help in any way he could. I worked so hard to make myself believe I loved him. And in a way, I know I did—do. One night he held me and things went farther than either of us intended. Just before we made love, he'd said, "You know I would never hurt you."

If John timed his call so that I would go to sleep with him on my mind, it worked. It was the first time in weeks that it was John's face and kisses I had on my mind as I fell asleep. I did know he would never hurt me and that said a lot, maybe a lot more than I'd been able to admit until my eyes closed with him saying, "You know I would never hurt you," repeating over and over.

Chapter Eight

Howler and I both slept on the couch. He was at my feet, and every time he turned or stretched, I woke up. At five, I got up, took a sponge bath—there was no way I was hopping into the shower—and brewed some coffee. At seven I was at Harry's 24 Hour Market picking up the twenty pound fresh turkey I'd asked them to hold, (I love turkey sandwiches and leftover dressing), and all the other items I'd need to replicate my mother's Thanksgiving dinner. Whenever I thought about the email that had sent me reeling the night before, I pushed it out of my mind. I picked up three bottles of great wine, red and white, and those little glass bottles of soda we all love.

By eight o'clock I was home, the day looming before me. I wish I'd told Caroline Kidston I would start painting for her before Thanksgiving. Time on my hands is a guaranteed anxiety breeder.

I set up my laptop and opened the file that housed my latest attempt at a novel. I wanted to do a meaningful piece of literary fiction, but whenever I started to write something prosaic and profound, I'd get to page fifty or thereabouts and then quit, as bored with it as I'm sure any potential editors or agents would be. I always ran through a litany of "what if's" that I'd been taught to use to generate ideas, but this time the "what ifs" turned into "What if I am the next victim?"

Images and words that connected to what had happened in the last few weeks bombarded me. I closed the file and opened a new one. Forget being literary, forget being published, I told myself to write something that would take my mind off Camphor, Michigan, and its next potential horror. Without thinking, I wrote the following:

Harriet had lived in Crabtree, Virginia, most of her life. Her sisters and brothers had long ago moved away, living tributes to their controlling father's determination to make doctors and lawyers of all five of his children. Only Harriet, the youngest, had let him down. A clerk at Crabtree Community Bank, she had been powerless to control her thirty-five-years of unceremonious living. A small house, an arthritic, lazy dog, and fifteen thousand in the bank represented the accumulation of a life devoted to fear. Harriet was lamenting all this as she looked out her window and saw the man run from the house next door. It was the knife in his hand that caused the breath to catch in her chest.

I didn't know if it was the blissful escape I felt writing about Harriet Hudacre (Love the last name!), or if it was that I felt a certain kinship, as if she were a part of me, but whatever it was, my fingers flew. The writing was far from Proust or Foucault, but I was totally engaged and wrote for hours without coming up for air. And all during that time, I never once considered the evils that might be swirling around me.

In what seemed a short time, page fifty loomed, and I was worried that I wouldn't be able to get past it on this book either. However, the feeling was different so maybe I had something I could finish. I stopped writing to fix lunch. My plan was to take Howler for a walk, get John and Javier pointed in the direction of my father's files, and then get back to Harriet.

"Howler, let's go for a walk," I said after I quickly put dishes in the dishwasher and wiped off the magnificent granite countertops my mother had put in just before she became ill.

When Howler and I stepped outside, I was surprised to be up to my ankles in snow. Howler, too, looked a bit worried about where his feet had gone. In my fear and preoccupation with all things deadly, I had totally missed the weather. I went back inside for my boots and pulled a not-too-happy-to-be-deep-in-snow Howler after me. We walked past the ladies' houses. No car in either driveway. Then I remembered it was Camphor Study Club day. The ladies were probably having a pre-Thanksgiving luncheon and listening to the latest gossip concerning the murders.

A few cars passed me. One was Whitey who waved too energetically, starting to slow down. I hurried up so I wouldn't have to talk to him. He took the hint and drove off.

The sun was on the snow and the air was so cold it had the same effect on me as sheets hung out in the fresh air, luring me into thinking it was devoid of pollution and toxicity. It was a great day. I could almost believe life would turn out okay. Then I let my mind drift to thoughts of Jory and the strange and wonderful sensations he evoked. His kisses were addictive. But maybe I had turned to him because he was there—and hot, very hot. Maybe it had been a way I could run from deeper, more serious feelings. The ladies had always thought I would end up with John. Should I have? Had I made a huge, life altering decision by turning him down when he asked me to marry him? But there was and always would be Caroline—and a baby. Oh, and on the other side, there was Jory's mother. Not exactly a fan.

To settle my head, I returned to the thinking about my Harriet story as Howler ran his nose through the snow in hopes that some delicacy was hiding from him. I considered what possible mystery my heroine might encounter. Was she a bit older, less hopeful me? Maybe she should be in her late twenties or early thirties. I wanted to create a woman who was her own person, lost in the mysteries that surrounded her—maybe she was me, but I intended to get to know Harriet and her world better. Who were her friends? I knew I was onto something because unlike so many other stories I'd started, this one was taking hold of me and also taking shape. What I was about to write actually held my interest. And I wanted to know how it ended. Harriet might be just what the doctor ordered to help me focus on something other than myself and my surroundings.

But no matter how hard I tried to stay away, murder always reared its bloody self. Why had the victims been targeted? I was tossing the question and its possible answers back and forth in my mind when I noticed that Howler and I had company. A figure followed about a block behind us. The person wore a hooded jacket, the hood pulled way down. He seemed to be pacing his steps with mine. I jerked Howler's leash to get him to speed up and picked up my pace, regretting that I was in the direction of the Nagels' house, a sparsely populated part of Cinnamon Street with few houses and enormous yards. We were blocks away from anyone I knew well enough to run to. I turned my head pretending to look at my dog, and out of the corner of my eye, I could see the figure beginning to jog. For a second my mind locked in fear.

As I saw the debris that had been the Nagel house, I knew there was no protection there. Howler pulled back on his leash and tried to get me to let him sit down. My wrist ached from jerking him to keep walking. Every time I gave him a yank, he turned and looked at me with his woebegone expression. I knew that within seconds the stalker would be upon us. Howler would have to get in gear whether he liked it or not. I knew Howler well enough to know that no matter how frightened I was by the stranger behind me, my dog would soon just sit down and refuse to move. When that happened, I was out of options.

My instinct was to cross the street and make a run for it, but most of the houses were unoccupied, their wealthy residents already in Florida establishing their six months of residency to assure lower taxes. I could hear my breathing. It was at warp speed. The figure was only half a block behind me now. Only one option remained. I turned and headed toward the figure, screaming gibberish at the top of my lungs and making wild and hideous facial expressions. I was now nearly face-to-face with the person who had stalked me.

"Ah ah! Ah ah!" I screamed at the top of my lungs, running on pure adrenalin. Then I started to kick the figure whose face was buried behind a scarf. I stuck out my tongue in spastic ways and rolled my eyes to the back of my head, a trick Earlene and I had perfected in eighth grade. I waited for what would surely be the hatchet that signaled my death. I knew Howler's low growl wouldn't be of much help.

Just as I was ready to fall in a heap, the hooded figure turned and sped away, racing around the first corner he came to. For some unfathomable reason, I was safe.

Howler was now sitting and looking at me as if I had totally lost my head—which was good because that was exactly what I had intended the stranger to think. I silently thanked the comedienne Carol Burnett for the trick. She's used it once when she was young and working in New York City. She said she'd been terrified by a man's stealthy footsteps one night when she left rehearsal. For a second she was as paralyzed as I'd been. She then turned and horrified her stalker by making a totally crazy, out-of-her-mind face. She showed the audience how she'd done it and had received gales of laughter. All I'd received was footsteps racing in the opposite direction, but that was wonderful to the nth degree.

I ran home, practically dragging Howler. As soon as I got to my front yard, I literally fell in the snow, weak but not totally panic stricken. I had taken control, gotten angry, and that seemed to ward off the panic.

But who was that person so eager to catch up to me? I knew nothing more than I had before. His head was nearly covered. He was taller than I, but not a whole lot heavier. Was it the same person who tied Howler in the basement and ransacked my house? I picked myself up from my yard. Howler, who was eating snow, followed along as I walked up my front steps. So this is what power feels like, I thought. At least it was power as I knew it. It had been a long time since I'd felt really in charge.

Perhaps another reason I felt so cocky was that I knew John and Javier would be arriving any minute. For sure, I wouldn't tell John Kidston what had just happened. Lately he had been far too eager to insinuate himself into my life. And he'd be right if he said I was stupid to head toward that part of the neighborhood alone.

"C'mon, fellow, let's go inside." When we got to the door, Howler pushed past me. Even he seemed to have gained a bit more confidence.

Chapter Nine

"E, feel free to do what you need to do once you point Javier and me toward your dad's files." John looked especially handsome in a brown leather jacket and tan slacks. I was glad he had called to say he and Javier would be an hour late because it gave me a few minutes to relax before they arrived.

"They're in the attic, and I'll need to lead you up there," I said.

"Good to see you again." In his state police uniform, Javier was all business.

"I really don't think there's anything here. How did you get the idea my dad's files might be helpful?" I led the men upstairs to the attic which has always scared me a bit.

"We can't really say," Javier said, "because it's part of the ongoing investigation and frankly might put you in some danger."

I thought back to the break in, and to what had happened just a few minutes before and considered telling Javier that perhaps I was already in great danger. But I didn't.

"Those are my dad's." I pointed to three tall files against the right wall of the dusty attic. Next to them were such treasures as my mother's crystal, silver and china. I made a note to one day clean them and bring them downstairs.

"Great. We may be a while." John took off his jacket and rolled up his sleeves. His thick, woodsy aftershave sent me back to a better, easier time in my life. "Got any coffee?" he asked before I could collect my feelings.

"I'll make you some." I hurried downstairs to brew some coffee. As soon as it was made, I could get back to the book I'd just started.

The coffeemaker slowly dripped a second round of coffee into the carafe as I got out my laptop. I was happy to get out of my world and back into Harriet's. Perhaps hers wasn't any safer than mine, but it was all hers. I didn't mind danger as much when it was pointed in someone else's direction. The doorbell was an unwelcome interruption. The visitor was even more unwelcome.

"Hello, Mrs. Esqueda." I was as nice as I could possibly be to the woman whose expression reeked disapproval, of me and of life in general.

"Is Junior here?" Her critical brown eyes quickly took in the living room and dining room. "I need to get in touch with him."

"I haven't seen him in a couple of days," I said regretfully.

"That's too bad," she said as if it wasn't. "His brother needs him to drive to the airport in Chicago tomorrow. Me, I don't drive, and my brother, Junior's uncle, was supposed to do it, but he broke his ankle today. The plans are changed."

"I'm so sorry to hear about your brother, but I'm sure you'll be happy to have your children home." I tried to be warm, but Mrs. Esqueda made it very difficult.

"How you know I'll be glad, huh?" she eyed me critically. "Besides, my daughters they can't be home. My daughter Lucy has to work at the hospital, and my other daughter Elena is a doctor in California. Just my son Ricardo from Colorado will be here. Oh, and Junior and Selma." Even in her Spanglish way of speaking, she made her point. Maybe I should start worrying why I hadn't heard from Jory. As far as Mama Esqueda was concerned, Selma was already part of the family. The men in my life came with entanglements. That was for sure.

"I had better go find Junior." She tromped to an SUV that had *Lawns by Esqueda* on it. Where was Jory? I hoped he wasn't playing me and that he didn't have a whole other life. Was he the kind of man who convinced women they were his one and only—all of them? No, that couldn't be Jory. Whatever he was doing, it had nothing to do with other women or murder. Right? And he wasn't interested in Selma, right?

I thought about warning Mrs. Esqueda that there might be a dangerous stranger in the neighborhood, but I didn't. If the murderer bumped into Mrs. Esqueda, heaven help him.

Again Harriet Hudacre and her enigmatic life helped. After I took the carafe to Javier and John, I quickly got back to my computer and into her story. I found myself wishing that I lived with Harriet in Crabtree, Virginia. I imagined it to be a small town like Camphor. But make believe, no matter how bloody and awful, was nowhere near what Camphor was experiencing. Harriet's lonely but comforting life was all I cared about as I wrote, and wrote, and wrote.

"We need to borrow this file." It was nearly ten p.m. when John and Javier finished in the attic. I hated to stop writing, even to see if they'd uncovered something helpful in solving the murder. I was suddenly tired of the whole thing.

"Anything you want—feel free to take it. What's in the file?" I studied the manila folder John held in his hand.

"We're not sure," John said. "But it's old information and coincides with the timeframe of the files stolen from Horace's office. We'll get it back as soon as we can."

A cell phone rang, and all three of us looked in the direction of our phones. It was John's.

"I'm just finishing up, Caroline," he whispered into the phone. "Sure, I'll pick some up on the way home. Tell him I said 'hello' and that I'll be home in an hour or so. No, I'm on my way and will be there as soon as I've run the errand."

By the way he was talking to her, I knew John hadn't told his wife where he was "finishing up."

"I have to get going," he turned suddenly edgy. "My wife's father is visiting us for Thanksgiving. He'd told us he couldn't make it until Christmas. He drinks an inordinately expensive gin, and we're running low." John didn't seem eager to deal with Caroline's arrogant, alcoholic father or delighted by the Thanksgiving surprise. I didn't care if her father was rich and famous, at John and Caroline's wedding, he'd been obnoxious and totally plastered, chasing every woman under thirty—including me. His visits to town had further painted him as a womanizer and drunk.

"I have to get going, too. I have some work at the police post before I go home. Lucy is keeping chicken enchiladas warm, and I don't want to miss them. Hey, we should have you and Jory over for them sometime." He smiled; John didn't.

"Sure," I said as I watched John become tense. Javier's seeing Jory and me as a couple gave me a great sense of relief. Surely Lucy would know if Selma were as much in the picture as Mama Esqueda wanted her to be. I regretted that Javier had commented about Jory and me in front of John, though. But he would have no way of knowing about John and my history.

Harriet shook from the fear that someone was watching her, wanting to shut her up permanently because of what she'd witnessed. Sitting there in the police station, she regretted that she'd ever told anyone about seeing the stranger leave the house. She wanted to go back to her boring, easy life at the bank.

"Are you Ms. Hudacre?" the most handsome man Harriet had ever seen was speaking to her. "I'm detective Homer Sloan but everyone calls me Scrap—I was a scrappy baby, I guess. Oh, maybe I was just junk?" He smiled and Harriet's heart and life lit up in a way she had never expected nor experienced. Scrap Sloan made every part of her go on alert. To what, she wasn't sure.

For the next two hours, I was totally engrossed in Harriet's suddenly turbulent life. I knew it read like a soap opera, but I also knew that there were hundreds of thousands of women who wanted the kind of escape from their mundane lives that Harriet's story— whatever it would turn out to be—might provide. After all, at the present time, I was admittedly one of those women. Only because the rumbling in my stomach reminded me I hadn't eaten in a very long time did I stop writing.

I was warming up a small frozen pizza and watching Howler devour his kibble when there was a familiar knock at the door. My own Scrap Sloan had arrived.

"I hear you experienced the return of Mama. I told her I had to be in class in Grand Rapids all day, but she forgot. Sorry. Did you survive it?"

"She wasn't bad," I lied. "Howler and I were wondering if you would ever darken our doorstep again."

"How could you doubt it, chica? You have had my heart for a long time. In fact I was going to stop by earlier but Kidston's car was here." The smile left

Jory's face. "Should I be worried? I know you and he were something a while ago, but you need to make me believe that's all over."

"Business. It was business. Your brother-in-law was here, too. They needed to go through---well, they needed to get some information. What have you been up to?"

"Law school. I go one whole day and one night a week. I have two years to go. Not fun."

"Can I get you some dinner?"

"Is that pizza I smell?" He headed toward the kitchen.

Soon Jory and I were sitting across from each other eating microwave pizza, drinking sodas, and trying futilely to keep our hands off each other.

"We have to stop meeting like this," he said when we were in my bed kissing, touching and demanding. Jory next to me, holding me tightly, made me feel that nothing could hurt me. Panic dissolved into warmth and passion. I was safe, totally safe in his arms and his life, I hoped.

"You know I'll be driving someplace during the day, and I will think about doing this, here with you. I think I have dreamed of you forever." Again Jory took over, and I floated with him past ecstasy and just around the corner from out-of-this-world.

"I didn't like it when I saw Kidston's car here," Jory repeated his theme hours later. "I hope you and the lawyer are truly old news."

"Not to worry. And I might ask you the same question about Selma. Your mother certainly wants me to believe there's something going on there."

"That NEVER was. It's a big dream in Mama's head. God I wish my dad was here for many reasons, mostly because he could control Mama. In her mind, Selma and I are meant for each other, but neither of us wants that. All we have in common is our heritage. She and I want different things. She wants babies and a man to take care of her. I can't be that guy. I like more independent, interesting women."

"Maybe if we're going to keep doing this, you need to let both your mother and Selma know I'm your lady."

"Done. And how 'bout you tell your friend John that I'm the man in your bed, ok?"

"Ok," I snuggled against him and into a safe, calm sleep. I was sure that I needed to let John know that he and I would never be anything more than friends. And I would do that as soon as I was absolutely sure it was true.

Jory was steamy, wonderful, and strong, and John was married. What kept me from an all out declaration of loyalty to Jory? Maybe it was the crazy times I was living in, and maybe it was something more. I didn't know. Pure and simple. I didn't know. I did know, however, whenever I tried to figure out exactly what to do, I felt panic begin to creep in. Instinct told me to stay put until I was absolutely sure that what I told Jory was the truth and that what Jory had told me was also the truth.

To my delight, Jory was sleeping next to me when I awoke early the next morning. "I started a book," I whispered to him as I gently shook him, knowing he had to make a drive to Chicago. "I like it."

"Oh, the painting lady is a writer, too, I forgot." He kissed my hair. "You are a woman of a great talent and mystery."

"Someone followed Howler and me when we were taking a walk."

He lifted his head. "Why didn't you tell me this sooner? E, you have to take all this seriously. Someone is telling you that you, too, are a part of all that's going on."

"I was so glad to see you that I forgot to tell you." I kissed him using my wiles to get back in his good graces.

"I'm going to call Javier before I take off for Chicago." He pushed aside my advances. "I don't think it is any coincidence that someone trailed you. I'm not letting anything happen to you." He kissed me and grabbed his shirt from my nightstand.

I dressed slowly, getting into my Michigan sweats and pulling my hair back into a makeshift ponytail. Jory certainly wasn't in love with me for my glamour girl looks, thank goodness.

"I can't get Javier on the phone, but I want to go over there anyway," Jory said. "Keep your doors locked. I'll give you a call when I'm on the road."

I was too tired to return to Harriet and her world, and there was no way I wanted to consider my schedule for painting the Kidstons' place so I started thinking about the next day—Thanksgiving. And I wished that Jory and I could celebrate it alone. I laughed to myself thinking that would never happen since the ladies were always in need of a place for the holidays. As long as they were around, they would be around me—and deep down I was grateful. I didn't want to think of a time when they wouldn't be there.

Howler started barking and my nerves shot to my eyebrows. It was barely eight o'clock. What had my dog so spooked? The doorbell sent me into an even greater tailspin. Surely a murderer wouldn't announce himself by ringing the doorbell. I looked out the window and was never happier to see Maurice Brunson.

"Hello, my dear." He gave me a light kiss on the cheek. "I am sorry it's so early, but I have these goodies for your Thanksgiving. It's my thank you for the beautiful job you did on my dining room. You know," he winked, "now we have to do something with that dark kitchen of mine. That ghastly gray doesn't work."

He handed me an enormous basket of cheeses, cheese spreads, wines, breads, crackers and cookies. There had to be hundreds of dollars worth of delicacies. On the very top was a check for the work. That, too, was far more than I'd expected.

"Maurice, you paid me nearly a thousand dollars more than the agreed price. And all these treats! The ladies are coming for dinner tomorrow. They will love them." He waved off my suggestion that he was overly generous. I dug deeper into the gift basket, and it revealed more tasty surprises, Godiva chocolate bunnies and Easter eggs as well as the Enstrom's Almond toffee I told him I loved. "Maurice, you are a treasure." I kissed his cheek.

"I packed some of those specialty coffees that Martha makes for us." He winked, walked into the living room, and sat down. "This is a lovely place. You know I don't think I've been here since your mother died. Can you believe it's been that long?" He took off his gloves and took both my hands in his. "You know, not a day goes by that I don't lament the death of your beautiful, perfect mother."

Tears fell down my cheeks. "I know. And I love that you loved her, too."

"I didn't mean to make you sad," he gently patted my back. "I just want you to know that we lost a gem when we lost her."

"And you, too, are a gem." I hugged him, hoping my tears didn't soak into his soft-as-cotton-cashmere coat. How lucky was Camphor to have a man as dear as Maurice!

"Well, let me get you some tea. I have a delicious raspberry herbal that I keep for Madge and Mignon."

"No, I do need to get home. I have a friend waiting for me. But I want you to have a lovely Thanksgiving. And if the ladies leave early, feel free to drop in at Chez Maurice. Martha's cooking, as you well know, is unparalleled."

"I appreciate your kind invitation. I really do, but I expect Madge and Mignon to stay well into the evening." I didn't tell him that it was Jory, not the ladies, who would keep me from leaving home. "Oh, by the way, Martha doesn't have a recipe for cinnamon apple salad, does she? I thought I had one but when I went to make it, I couldn't find it. So here I am with ingredients, but no recipe."

"I am happy to say that Martha has a cherry cinnamon one that is mouth-watering with those little red cinnamon candies plopped into cherry jello, and she also has one with dark cherries and cream cheese. I absolutely adore both of them. I'll email them to you as soon as I get home. I'm not much with the computer but the friend waiting for me has a gift."

"I love you," I said as I hugged him one more time. "You are wonderful! Come back when you can stay, ok?"

"Soon! I promise. Now I must be off."

"Well, Howler, aren't we glad that it was just Maurice?" I petted my dog who still seemed to be withholding judgment.

"Well, guy, who would have taken you for a homophobe?" I gave him a dog biscuit, put on the fire, and settled back to organize the recipes. Within an hour, Maurice emailed the salad recipes. I made a quick run to the grocery store to pick up the ingredients, as well as a few things I'd forgotten before.

Though I was late getting home, and since I was going to do the stuffing in the slow cooker, I did all the preliminary preparations for both the stuffing and the sweet potato casserole, the Jello salads, the make ahead mashed potatoes (with both sour cream and cream cheese) and pie crusts. I would wait until later to finished the pies, and in the morning I would prepare the turkey with my mother's recipe for herb butter.

My mother was a taskmaster in the kitchen as I was growing up, correcting me when I forgot to carefully measure and clean up after every dish. I looked around at the kitchen when I was done and knew if she weren't already dead the sight would have killed her. Strewn over the counter were empty cans, ripped-open Jello cartons, and splotches of liquid. Sorry, Mama, but it's done, right? In truth, I am a good cook when I want to be, but I remember too many times with my mother standing behind me, correcting me, to really love working in the kitchen.

I missed Jory and though he called from the road when I was cleaning the silver and getting the house ready, I felt empty. It had been over four years since my mother died but I still missed her—and I missed my father, too, though he'd been gone far longer. I hemmed the new long skirt I'd bought for the holidays and tried to write and then to read. I couldn't accomplish either. I drifted for most of the day, going through the motions of setting the table and washing the good china.

When Jory didn't return, I went to bed after ten— pies baked and table set with my mother's Limoges. I also used her crystal and some wine glasses the ladies gave me for my birthday. Oh, and I put out my mother's sterling, which looked a bit as if it should have been more meticulously polished. I made a note to do a more thorough cleaning before the Christmas dinner. Everything sat on my mother's elegant ivory tablecloth, which she'd used at all our festive occasions.

At these moments, I regretted I couldn't see more of my dad in the picture, but he was a tall, quiet man who saw his duty as taking care of his wife and little daughter. I didn't know him well, but heard from a great many others that he was honorable and highly-respected. When he died far too soon, I think he took a lot of my mother with him. She lost her laughter.

That night my mind raced with too many thoughts. I fought to get to sleep, but Howler was snoring hours before I finally fell asleep. Tired as I was, I woke several times, not being able to remember what I'd been dreaming but with a sense of dread.

Very, very late, I heard a noise in my room that would have scared me to death had I not heard Jory whisper, "Shhh, it's just me, babe," as he slid his warm body next to mine.

"Where have you been," I whispered as I turned toward him. "I started to worry."

"Don't worry about what I'm going to say. Everything is all right. Javier was shot, but he's home—just a surface wound in the arm."

And as frightened as I was to hear what Jory said, I needed his body more. I went to him and became so much a part of him that I couldn't imagine being with another man. In the morning I would hear all about what happened to Javier, but at that moment all that mattered was Jory—and me.

Chapter Ten

Jory was gone by the time I woke at eight. There was no coffee perking and no answer to the question of what had happened to Javier. The ladies would be arriving a little after two, and there was still a Thanksgiving meal to get on the table.

I stuffed and put the turkey in the oven even before I made my first cup of coffee, this time a latte from the big expensive espresso machine that had been another birthday present from the ladies. I used the syrup I'd bought at Starbucks and came as close to a gingerbread latte as I could hope to. Finally, I turned on the TV and sat down with a second latte.

The news about Javier was first.

"State Police Trooper Javier Rodriguez was shot at approximately nine o'clock last night as he investigated a suspected burglary in Camphor. Officer Rodriguez is reportedly listed in good condition. We have no further information at the present time, but as soon as we do, we will pass it on."

The announcement begged more questions than it answered. Who was burglarized and why? I went to the computer to see if I could find out, but the media had obviously been told to put a hold on revealing any more information to the public. I was glad I already knew that Javier had been released from the hospital and was resting comfortably at home. I felt sorry that he'd be spending Thanksgiving incapacitated, but at least he was alive, more than could be said for several other Camphorites.

Next, I printed out names in a calligraphy-like font on cardstock to use for place cards. I knew it was silly, but Mignon holds on to a gentler, more gracious time, and I knew if I had place cards at the ladies' seats at least Mignon would appreciate it. Even if there would only be three people and they all knew each other, the cards would make the table look formal and elegant. My mother must be smiling.

Howler, no more a morning person than I, sat by my feet waiting for his beloved dog biscuits.

"You are a greedy Gus," I said when he let out a surprisingly large belch after I fed him his "cookie."

Great smells filled the air, Crockpot stuffing, turkey, all the pies, and even another pot of coffee brewing. Only Mignon and I would eat the apple pie because Madge was a pumpkin pie devotee. I was proud of myself. Everything was underway. There was even a little time to write.

I'd left my laptop on the kitchen island the night before so stood as I clicked on the Harriet file and started to read. As I reread the draft, I had confidence that it was as good as anything I'd read in the genre. Maybe if I continued with the same energy I'd put into it already, I had a chance of getting an agent and getting it published. It wasn't the great American novel I'd been encouraged to write at Michigan, but it was entertaining, and there was a lot to be said for escapist reading. I'd certainly read my share.

My fingers flew as I added exciting scenes to the mystery. Harriet was a loveable mix of most of the people in my life. She had Mignon's manners and Madge's curiosity. She also had my tendency to run from rather than to life. I wrote furiously for the next couple of hours, stopping only to throw Howler another dog biscuit and pour cups of coffee. I had over twenty pages when I forced myself to call a halt at eleven thirty, and, best news of all, I didn't want to stop. I had mentally outlined what was coming next. Harriet was heading into uncharted, troubling territory. But since it wasn't me, I felt no panic, only excitement.

When I checked my email, there were two waiting for me. The first was another salad recipe from Maurice: a delicious strawberry and cream cheese one that I remembered from a lawn party at his house. The other one had a heading that read: *Girl, You Better Listen.* I immediately deleted it. I would not let that monster into my thoughts. Today was going to be a great day. I would make sure of it.

As if to support my determination, Jory called. "I miss you," I told him, "but you need to tell me what happened to Javier."

"I don't want to involve you any more than you already have been."

"I'm involved, ok? John and Javier found a file in my dad's business papers that they think might have something to do with the murders."

"I don't know anything about the file," Jory said, "but I know that Javier was checking out a call. Someone reported a burglar at Harvey Barnes' home. When Javier got there, he was fired on. A neighbor called it in because Harvey's wife has been staying with her sister in Grand Rapids. Now do you feel included?"

"A little." But I was also a little less brave, wishing he had been able to trust me more, to let me in on what he knew. Why in the heck had Harvey Barnes been murdered? Was he connected to the other murders or was it a payback from some angry felon he'd dealt with?

"I'll get out of Mama's as fast as I can and get to you."

I loved hearing him say it, but I still wasn't sure how the ladies felt about my dating the gardener's son, especially when they still held onto the hope that I would end up with John Kidston. "If you leave her house too early, what will your mama say?"

"Mama and I are kind of on the outs. Unbeknownst to me, she invited Selma's folks for today's meal. I told her that it was a bad idea, and since then she's given me the silent treatment, as only Mama can. Not to worry. I'll patch it up, and soon Mama will see how foolish she's been. My brother Ricardo is going to his girl's in Rockford tonight. I'll take off when he leaves."

"Well, I'm thrilled. Get over here as soon as you can."

"E!" Mignon was yelling at me through the door as she rang the bell. "Let me in!"

"Are you ok?" I opened the door fearing the worst.

"No, I'm not ok!" She had driven her car, parked wildly in front of my house, but had been in such a rush she had neglected a jacket or boots.

"Come in here. I'm going to get some tea to warm you up as you tell me what has you in such a tizzy."

"Tizzy! Who wouldn't be in a tizzy with that animal living next door."

"Oh," I said boiling the water for some of the holiday mix of teas in Maurice's basket of goodies. "You and Madge are at it again."

"Not Madge—that beast she brought from Paws with Jaws or something. It's nothing more than a tramp dog, and it's ugly as hell."

"Animal Rescue. She got Hannibal from Animal Rescue." I bit my tongue because it was obviously no laughing matter to Mignon.

"I don't care. It has to go. It poops pyramids! You should see what that animal is doing to my backyard."

"Madge told me that she intends to put up a fence. She just can't get it done until after Thanksgiving. And

I'm sure if you tell her what's going on, she'll make sure Hannibal stays in his own yard."

"Oh, E, don't give that creature a name! It humanizes that monster. Did you ever see anything uglier! And smelly! My gawd it is the smelliest thing in town."

"But Madge seems to love him," I said defensively. Poor Hannibal couldn't help how he looked.

"Seems to love him—that is the most pathetic understatement for the way she treats that putrid canine. She has time for nothing but tossing a ball to him—and that's truly a travesty since the dog sits there and watches Madge's decrepit self throw it and then hobble to retrieve it. The dog does nothing but sleep and shit, but that doesn't seem to matter to Dumbo. Oh, listen to my language! She has me so upset."

"It's a phase. Madge is just getting him used to things. Then she'll have time for you."

"Me? You think this is about my wanting Madge to spend time with me! Oh that's not it at all." She protested too much. "I just wanted that hideous, furry corpse out of our neighborhood."

"Well, it's not going to happen. Madge loves Hannibal too much. And I think he's kind of cute. You should try to make friends with him. That will please Madge, and you'll feel better about Hannibal."

"Oh, I shouldn't have come here!" Mignon rose to leave. "You are all soppy-eyed over that gardener, and Madge has gone bonkers for something that should have been put out of its misery long ago."

"Let's change the subject," I said, feeling myself bristling at her crack regarding Jory. "Do you know any reason that someone might want to root through my dad's old files regarding the Nagels?"

"Why?" Mignon eyed me suspiciously. "What would old files have to do with anything?"

"I'm not sure, but there are files missing from the attic, and they could be related to the Nagel family. Yesterday Javier Rodriguez, a state trooper and Jory's brother-in-law, was attacked at Harvey Barnes' place."

"I'm sure they're not connected, dear. "Now, tell me how I can help you get ready."

She was definitely eager to change the subject. "Well, sit here and talk to me. I'm just going to get out the sparkling wine and grape juice. Madge should be here soon." As Mignon let out a low groan, I hastily added. "You look gorgeous. Is that a new outfit?"

"It is," she brightened. "I bought it in Ann Arbor last week." She ran her tapered fingers over the soft gray wool slacks and the magenta cashmere sweater.

"Good choice." I felt conspicuous in my knit gray, ankle length skirt, and the wine-colored silk blouse I'd worn too often at holidays. "I need to go shopping," I said. "I seem to be wearing the same things over and over again. The skirt's new, though, do you like it?"

"I do, but with the best legs in town, why are you wearing a long skirt? Maybe you and I should go shopping. Let me get you some things," she said.

"Oh, that's so sweet but I have plenty of money to get some clothes." And I did. I'd stockpiled my painting checks and, of course, there was always what my parents left me. The unintended and unwelcome consequence of losing them so young was a pile of money that was reinvested in very secure funds. "I'll get some things. It would be fun to go on a shopping trip, though," I added so that her feelings wouldn't be hurt.

"Now that there's a man in your life, you might want to do just that." The look on her face asked a question I had no desire to answer.

"Maybe. Could you set another place at the table? I did tell you that Jory might be here for dinner, didn't I?"

"That's nice," Mignon said as if it weren't.

Mignon was in the family room watching HGTV when Madge arrived.

"Happy Thanksgiving!" she shouted. "Look who I brought. I just couldn't leave him alone on Thanksgiving, could I?" She gave a tug on a rhinestone leash, and there was Hannibal, less smelly but looking wilder and more woolly everywhere but his torso, which was still nearly bald.

"Doesn't he be boootiful," Madge cooed to her canine misfit. "I had him bathed at Pampered Pups."

"Well, I think he looks lovely," I said thinking that Hannibal was the first animal I remembered who didn't seem to improve with grooming. Every strand of his wiry hair headed in a different direction, and the naked spots looked almost reptilian.

"Mignon said that you didn't want me to bring him for Thanksgiving, but I knew once you saw how great he looks, you would love having him around." Her eyes shot a dart at Mignon who had wandered into the foyer, holding a huge glass of wine.

"You know I love dogs," I said helping Madge tug a terrified Hannibal into the living room. "Let me get Howler and put him upstairs." I had been listening to my own dog's low growl that telegraphed he was not eager for companionship. I grabbed some dog biscuits before I took him upstairs to shut him in my room. I put half a dozen on the bed beside him. I also made a mental note to let him out somewhere between dinner and dessert.

"I'm getting a dog," Mignon was saying when I walked back into the room.

"That's the funniest thing I've heard. You would never allow a dog in that palace of yours. You don't even allow dust to collect there." Madge was dressed in hot pink slacks with an ill-chosen purple polyester top. For some ungodly reason, she had an orange bow at the top of her hair. She looked as weird as Hannibal. She was totally Madge, though, and I totally loved her. When I'd been too exhausted to hold my mother's head one more time when she threw up, Madge did. Both she and Mignon were there in the worst times of my mother's illness, but Madge did the dirty work. Mignon paid to have it done. Either way, I was eternally grateful.

"Well, you just wait and see what I come up with. You have turned our neighborhood into a home for wayward and ugly animals. I will get one that makes it beautiful."

Madge's face was as orange as her bow.

"I think dinner is just about ready," I said as Mignon reached for the gin and Madge started to reach for Mignon. "Maybe we'd better put off any more drinks until after we've eaten. I have wine."

"Oh, my dear, this table is as lovely as your mother's holiday dinners." Mignon paid me the ultimate compliment as she entered the dining room and placed herself at one end of the table. I sat in the middle so Madge could sit at the other end. I'd keep them too far away to hurt each other.

"Jory is coming, but we won't wait," I said. "He doesn't expect to be here before dessert. That was his brother-in-law who was shot the other night."

"Good wine," Mignon said with a slight slur to her words. "And damn good stuffing, E." She hadn't heard a word I said and that might be just as well. "I wish you'd let me bring more than rolls."

"Rolls are fine. The town tells horror stories about the meals you tried to cook." Madge was uncharacteristically mean.

"Rolls are plenty, Mignon, and these are delicious," I nervously stuffed a chunk in my mouth. I didn't need a food fight at Thanksgiving. "Did you get them at Larva's?"

"Larva's," Madge giggled. "I can't get over the name of our bakery. Larva's. What a picture that puts in my mind, little worms in and out."

She, too, had one glass of wine too many. I should have rethought the wine. "Madge, these potatoes are delicious." I practically choked on them as I tried to keep her mind occupied with something other than Larva's nearly oxymoronic name.

"I would have brought more, but I caught Hannibal eating them," she said. "I think I got all the ones he had been licking and threw them out. Oh, well, it's not like he has germs."

"Madge, you are an idiot," Mignon stood and was as purple as her sweater. "You are feeding us the leftovers of that creature's scavenging. You are as nuts as Cissy Weatherbee was before she died."

"Hey, don't you be insulting Duane's relatives."

"I wasn't," Mignon momentarily lost her balance and sat back in her chair. "I was insulting you."

"It's Thanksgiving," I said. "Both of you stop. I went to a lot of work, and I expect you to be on your best behavior or no pie. And I want to thank the two of you for being here—for being my family."

At the family part, Madge and Mignon both looked a little shamefaced. Good. They should feel guilty about acting like ten-year-olds. At that moment, I got a scent of something awful, something from under the table. Something from Hannibal.

"That is the worst smell I have ever experienced!" Mignon jumped from the table knocking over her chair. "Something inside that dog is dying."

"Oh shut up!" Madge dove under the table. "Are you all right, baby. Oh, I think it's the sweet potatoes. Maybe he got more than I thought."

Another shot of awful told us all that Hannibal was definitely not well.

"He does seem to be sick." I bent down to see how Madge and her old bones were coming with Hannibal. The smell was so putrid, I had to get out of there and return to a green-looking Mignon.

"Oh I don't think I should have given him the bourbon balls either." Madge said, still under the table. "I bought them for you, E, but I ate half a dozen, and then he started begging. You know he doesn't get very excited about anything, but he wanted the candy so much so I gave him a couple."

"A couple?" I asked watching Hannibal open his mouth and hurl a brown mass onto my plush rose carpeting. "Define a couple." I raced to get some wet paper towels and a bucket.

"Well, maybe eight or ten—no more than ten, though."

"You absolute nincompoop!" Mignon started to pull dishes off the table and carry them to the kitchen. "You bring a dog that should be pushing up daisies to a dinner where he is not wanted, and now he proceeds to die in front of us."

"He's not dying." Madge and I were both wiping up vomit slower than Hannibal was producing it. "Do you think he's dying, E?"

"I don't think he's dying, but I do think we need to get him to the vet. Mignon, will you stay here while I drive Madge to the Emergency Animal Hospital?" I was glad Jory was late. One of the many things we had yet to discuss was how strong his stomach was. Hannibal's performance might make Jory as nauseous as I was beginning to feel. "Jory should be here any minute. Just let him know what happened and tell him I'll be back as soon as I can, ok?"

I left Mignon looking dazed and confused as she took the bucket from me and prepared to scrub the carpet, perhaps for the first time in her life.

Madge and I put Hannibal in the backseat of my car. "Do you think he'll be all right back there?" Madge focused on Hannibal as I set a new land speed record driving to the vet's.

"I'm sure he'll be all right. We're doing the right thing, though. A doctor needs to look at him."

When we got there, several cars were already in the parking lot, but the waiting room was empty. Soon a young vet tech walked in to take Hannibal's vitals. Madge's geriatric pet perked up a bit and quit tossing his bourbon balls once we got inside the building.

"He seems better don't you think?" Madge said petting his static-electric hair. "I think he'll be all right."

"He will," I squeezed her hand.

The young female veterinarian who x-rayed Hannibal and checked him over said she felt sure that he had relieved himself of what was causing his discomfort. Madge and I could vouch for the fact that he had done so massively and frequently. But the veterinarian said she wanted to keep him overnight because he was an "older" dog and because he might be a bit dehydrated. I drove a teary, guilt-ridden Madge back to my house. Mignon's car was still parked in front, right next to Jory's. Oh oh.

"E, we have had the most wonnerful time," Mignon was sitting next to Jory, her hand holding his. "This dear boy has helped me clean—clean—the , what was it we were cleaning, dear?" She patted his face as Jory sat looking like the cat who swallowed the canary.

"We cleaned the floor, Mrs. Dalton."

"Mrs. Dalton! Oh noooooo, we are toooo good friends for that. I'm going to propose you for the country club—the one I belong to—"

"Are you just going to sit there and embarrass yourself?" Madge asked dabbing at her eyes. "Don't you even want to know about Hannibal?"

Mignon stopping fawning over Jory and looked at Madge wiping away tears. "Well," she said sitting up straight. "It's never easy to lose an animal, but that one was half dead when you got it."

"Mignon!" I said.

"Hannibal is not dead!" Madge shouted. "He's fine—just staying at the vet's overnight. You are a horrible old witch." Madge's sobs were loud, nearly inhuman.

"Sorry." Mignon giggled and went back to ogling Jory.

"Mignon, I think we'd better get you to bed. You're going to sleep here," I said thinking that I didn't want her in her own house as drunk as she was. If someone broke in, she'd never hear him. "Jory, can you help me get her to a guest room?"

"I'd better get home." Madge started toward the door.

"You stay, too," I commanded. Suddenly I had a need to keep us all safely under the same roof. "That way you and I can go get Hannibal first thing in the morning. You can stay in my parents' old bedroom. It will be like a slumber party. Just stay down here until we get Mignon to bed."

"I guess you and I aren't going to be having a slumber party," Jory kept his voice low as we were slipping a dead-to-the-world Mignon into the antique four poster bed with the lush comforter.

"I know," I said regretfully, "but they are both such a mess."

"I was mostly kidding," his smile was full of compassion. "But speaking of messes, I've got to see Mama so it will probably be best if I sleep at my own house anyway. I was late because she and I got into it. My dad would kill me for giving her a hard time, but he wouldn't be too happy with her either."

"My name didn't happen to come in the fight with your mother, did it?"

"Maybe—a little, but it's more than that. I'm going to move into my own place soon, and she thinks I should live with her forever. I'm going to tell the guy who's doing the remodel to put a rush on it. Men over thirty definitely should not live with their mothers. I hope you like the house. I think it looks homey, and the workshop in the back is great—as is the master bedroom." He kissed me long and hard.

"Did Selma's name come up in the argument?" I wasn't going to give up, even with his wondrous kisses.

"She's no bigger a problem for me than John Kidston is for you." I could tell he said it to get my reaction. I maintained my best poker face.

"That's good." I said and decided to change the subject just as Madge entered the room.

"Can we go get Hannibal first thing in the morning? I know he'll be afraid without me and with all those strange dogs."

I didn't have the heart to tell her that there was no stranger dog than Hannibal. "First thing—after coffee." I led her upstairs.

"Oh my gosh, did you eat?" I asked when I rejoined Jory. "Let me get you something before you take off. "

"Mama fed me and then Mignon did too. I'm fine. In fact I'm great with you right where you belong." He took me in his arms. "As Mrs. Dalton was helping herself to the wine, I helped myself to your terrific turkey, dressing, potatoes and pie. I loved the apple pie. Your gifts are boundless." He put his strong hands on my waist and pulled me into him. I was as greedy for his kisses as he was for mine and didn't want it to stop.

"If I don't leave now, I'll never leave," he said.

I gave Jory a long, hungry goodnight kiss. Then he went to confront his angry Mama, and I went to toss and turn in a cold, lonely bed. And for a moment, I celebrated the fact that for most of the day I had given no thoughts to murder or murderers.

Madge is an early riser and her determination to get Hannibal made her an even earlier riser. She'd already made coffee when I stumbled downstairs a little before 7. "I called the vet and Hannibal is up and friskier than ever." She was literally beaming as she handed me the coffee. "But she doesn't want us to pick him up until this afternoon. Is that ok?"

"Sure." The coffee was strong—frighteningly so.

"The veterinarian said that she is going to put Hannibal on a very strict diet and that I shouldn't feed him anything not on the list she'll give me."

"That's probably a very good idea. Bourbon balls may be too rich for dogs." I put the coffee aside and made a mental note to leave early so that I could get a latte on our way to pick up Hannibal. Madge's coffee was strong enough to grow hair on my teeth.

Mignon came down before eight o'clock. She looked as if she had been professionally groomed—hair and skin flawless.

"Well," she said, "how is he?"

"Better." Madge didn't look at Mignon as she answered.

"You must feel very relieved." Mignon's tone was almost conciliatory.

"I am," Madge snapped.

"You know," Mignon said, "if E doesn't mind, I'd like to take you to the veterinarian to pick him up. We could stop at the pet store on our way and get him some toys. I'm a little serious about getting a dog myself so maybe you could give me some advice."

I couldn't believe my ears but said nothing in case it was all a glorious dream. The look on Madge's face said she, too, was having a hard time believing Mignon was for real.

"Would you mind, E?" Madge asked me.

"Not really. I mean, I can't wait to see Hannibal all well and happy, but I bet he'd love the toys that Mignon is going to get him."

"And I might get him something else, too," Mignon winked at me.

"I'm ready when you are," Madge said after we'd finished our eggs and toast breakfast and put the dishes in the dishwasher. "Did I tell you I'm going to have a trainer come to the house? I think I could train Hannibal to be a watchdog."

"A trainer is a good idea," Mignon said. "Maybe we could share one."

"Well," Madge said, "then we should get home and get changed. I have a dog book that has all the breeds and tells about each one. And I think the pet store has dogs from animal rescue. You might even get one as good as Hannibal."

"Oh, I doubt I'll be that lucky," Mignon said helping Madge on with her jacket.

"Don't forget to check your houses when you get home. If anything is out of the ordinary," I said, "come right back here."

"We will." They said in happy unison.

After they left, I wondered if there was something wrong with Mignon—perhaps a stroke coming on—and that could account for the about face in her behavior. I chose the other possibility, though, that she really liked Madge and knew she had hurt her friend's feelings. There were limits and Mignon is gracious and smart enough to know when she assaults both people's feelings and the rules of propriety.

Friday. It was Friday! I'd told Caroline Kidston I would start the baby's room today. How could I have put that so completely out of my mind? I was late!

It seemed weeks rather than days since I'd assembled my equipment and slipped into my work clothes. Thank goodness my painter's whites were clean. Caroline Kidston would want her painter to be officially dressed. My paints and brushes were in the trunk so within half an hour I was on my way to Kidstons'. I wanted to get the job done as soon as possible because the sooner I started, the sooner I would be done with the whole thing.

John met me at the door. "I-I- would stay to talk," he stammered, "but Maurice is in the hospital and I have to get over there."

"Maurice! What happened?"

"Someone beat him up early this morning. He'll be all right, but he will be in the hospital for a few days and needs me to take care of some things for him."

"Do they know who did it?" I thought of the handsome strangers always wandering in and out of Maurice's mansion.

"He got a look at someone, but the person was wearing a hood. He was just pushed around a bit but so terrified that Glen Newell wanted him to stay for observation."

My next question caught in my throat. "A hood?" My stalker had worn a hood.

"Yes. Well," he said, "have fun painting. I'll warn you that Caroline is not in a great mood."

"Oh, she feels badly for Maurice?"

"Caroline? She's not worried about Maurice," he said as he grabbed his attaché, "she's worried about the cocktail party we're throwing tonight for a few of her father's Harvard buddies."

"Oh—John, before you go, do you think it was the murderer or someone connected to the murders who hurt Maurice?" My hands started to shake.

"I do," he said. "Maurice told the police that the man had an axe and was ready to use it when he heard the burglar alarm go off. That seemed to spook him and he left."

"Oh, it's never going to end." Without thinking, I leaned into him.

"E!" Caroline Kidston had entered the foyer, and her face wore the look of pure hatred.

Chapter Eleven

"I was telling E about Maurice, Caroline." John was almost penitent. "I'll call you after I've been to the hospital." He went to kiss his wife, but she turned her cheek.

"Come in," Caroline commanded.

"Let me get my stuff," I said and ran back to the car to grab a ladder.

I made three trips from my car to the house without one offer of help from Caroline. In her very expensive dress and shoes, however, I knew that her help couldn't be much.

"What were you and John really talking about?"

"Just what he told you. I still can't believe that Maurice was hurt."

"Not badly." She was cold as the snow starting to collect on the lawns and sidewalks outside.

"Did you have a good Thanksgiving?" I tried to make small talk since she was still standing there, watching me put my buckets, rollers and ladders on a drop cloth.

"Good enough, I guess. We went to dinner with some of Daddy's old friends at the club. I haven't been feeling well enough to cook. Then John had work to do. Always work, work, work with him." She shot me a look that let me know she had revealed more than she intended.

"My dad was a lawyer too," I said, my mouth going as fast as my beating heart. "He went into banking because he was afraid he wouldn't have time for the family."

"John may just have to think about that, too. I don't intend to be the only one raising the kid. Well, is there anything else you'll need? I have a board meeting. I'll be back later."

"John said you're having a party. I'm afraid this room will look pretty bad for a few days."

"Oh, we're not having it here," she sneered. "We'll be at the club. Daddy loves it."

Bliss. With Caroline gone, I could relax. I could also consider what had happened to Maurice. Another Brunson had suffered an attack. A good detective à la Hercule Poirot would have started long ago to think about who would profit from the Brunson family's being offed. Then I remembered that Harvey, too, had been killed and he was not a Brunson. Maybe there was a connection, though, that I wasn't aware of. I would nose around Whitey to find out what he knew. In the meantime, I would live on the verge of panic.

I usually work fast, but I was exceptionally speedy as I prepped and primed the Kidstons' two rooms in record time. The faster I painted the less likely I would have to spend any time with the queen of awful. I put Kilz on the walls in both rooms and then made the cuts near the ceiling that I pride myself on. I'm really good. Everyone says that I'm the best interior painter in the area. It's a compliment that I don't think would have made my mother particularly proud, but I feel good about it nevertheless.

It wasn't easy. The paint she had picked was even worse than I remembered. My arms ached from rolling it to a thin enough consistency. And Overtons' paints would have been so much better. Steve had a lovely off-white that would put this paint with its arrogant, pretentious name to shame.

My cell rang, and I answered it only to give my aching arms a rest.

"Miss me?" It was Jory.

"Always."

"Let's do something about that. I'm not taking no for an answer. Tonight let's get a great steak with some wine at The Fireside and see what happens next, ok?"

"Ok!" Playing coy has never been my style— sometimes to my disadvantage and my mother's shame.

Jory's call had fueled me. I was totally done with one room and out the door before Caroline returned. On the table I'd left a note saying that I'd be back to finish the baby's room in a day or so and that it would be a gift from me so I only billed for the room I'd finished. I didn't care what Caroline thought. John was an old friend.

The minute I got home and opened the door, Howler raced out. Snow or no snow, he had a job to get done. I checked the mail and my messages.

"You better not be doing anything tonight," Suzi's voice was barely audible, all fuzzy. "I'm on my way, and there's no stopping me. I just read about another murder in Camphor, and I have to see my roomy in person." Click.

I dialed her phone but got a, "Hi, this is Suzi. I'm not available right now. Please leave your name and number because I'm eager to talk to you."

I dialed Jory, also getting his machine. "Hi, this is E I can't believe I have to say this, but I can't go to dinner, and other things, tonight. My college roommate has left a message that she's on her way here. Though I want you to meet her, tonight is probably not the night. Love, Me." I'd hung up before I realized I'd said love. I don't think I'd ever told anyone, even John, that I loved him. Love had been reserved for my parents and the ladies.

The phone rang as I was making myself a cup of hot chocolate.

"E, come over here. Right now, please." Mignon's voice sounded needy enough that I grabbed my jacket and left my hot chocolate on the counter before I race-walked to her home, which was elegance personified. Suzi wouldn't be there for a couple of hours. She'd probably left right after work if I knew Suzi. Still, Chicago was an hour behind us so it would be at least nine before she arrived.

"Well, my dear, I have done it."

My first reaction was that Mignon had bought tickets for the 'round the world cruise she'd threatened to take. I couldn't have been more wrong. The answer to the question of what she was talking about was a tiny cotton ball on her lap.

"This is Tiffany, and I just bought her at animal rescue. Madge helped me find her."

"Oh she is darling." I didn't have to lie one bit. What Mignon held in the palm of her hand was a tiny ball of white mohair with black eyes.

"She's a purebred Maltese. Madge insisted we go to Animal Rescue before we went to the pet store and I found this precious little girl. What a blessing Madge is."

I studied Mignon's eyes to see if her pupils were severely dilated. "I need to talk to you, friend to friend." I sat down next to Mignon who still held Tiffany. "As long as I've known you, you haven't liked animals. Oh, you tolerate Howler, but you never wanted one. What's really going on?"

"Madge." Mignon said.

"You feel a competition with her?" I asked. "She has a dog and you need a dog?"

"No. I wouldn't get a dog just to compete. I'm not that foolish, my dear. The other night at your house, when that creature of hers was so ill, I saw what that dog means to her, and I became frightened about what will happen to Madge when the animal expires. And let's be real, E dear, the dog is dead dog walking."

"So you got Tiffany for Madge?" I said.

"For both of us. I need to hug something besides that old lothario Glen, and Madge will need something to love when Hannibal is no longer with us—which may be sooner rather than later."

"It's not like Hannibal has one foot in the grave," I said. Mignon's look told me she didn't think I was a good judge of dog mortality. "This is a picture pup, Mignon." I couldn't resist picking up little Tiffany. "You'll love having a dog."

"I hope that thing next door doesn't eat her." Mignon petted her fluff of fur.

"Only if you feed it to him. Hannibal is not an aggressive dog."

"That is not a dog," she looked in the direction of Madge's.

"Do you know that Maurice is in the hospital?" I asked.

"What happened?" Mignon looked stunned.

"He's fine, but he might not have been. Someone attacked him."

"Oh gawd. We stopped being close long ago, but I never would want anything to happen to him. Oh, this is awful. Brunson heirs are on somebody's hit list."

"Well, he's going to be fine," I didn't want to upset her anymore than I had. "Hey, tell me how you got this little doll."

"Well, Madge and I went to the shelter before we picked up her leviathan. And this little pooch was there along with many others that they were trying to get adopted."

"But she looks purebred. I didn't know they had those."

"Oh, it's a sad story. Her mother was an abused dog, pregnant with a litter when they rescued her from a house at the edge of town. Some husband who was divorcing his wife took the little dog and was beating her. Well, in the fire, Animal Rescue saved her and several other dogs. They didn't know she was pregnant. The mother has been adopted by a wonderful family," Mignon, not an animal lover to my knowledge, was crying. "But there were three puppies. Tiffany, her full name is Mignon's Precious Tiffany, was the runt and the last. I told them I'd take her right then. It cost me nearly a thousand dollars because when I went to pay the $150 they were asking, Madge said, 'C'mon, Mrs. Rich Bitch, you can do better than that.'"

"But aren't you glad you did it?" I asked.

"My family did not hold onto its money by writing thousand dollar checks to animal shelters," she sniffed. "But I will say that Tiffany is well worth it."

"Well, I think this is great. You need Tiffany, and it sounds like she needs you, too." It didn't escape me that since murder victims had been piling up in Camphor, Madge and Mignon had rushed into getting dogs, and I had rushed into bed with Jory. Camphor's calamities had taken a toll on us all.

"Welcome to Tiffany, but I better get home. My roommate Suzi is coming!" I gave both Mignon and Tiffany quick kisses.

"Oh, please let me take the two of you to the club tomorrow night. I haven't seen her since your mother's funeral. We'll even ask the lady next door, if she can leave that enormous stink bomb for a couple of hours!"

I started to tell her why that wouldn't work, but Glen Newell—walking straight into the house as if he owned the place—interrupted us.

"Well, there she is," he said not to Mignon but to Tiffany, now perched contentedly on her mistress's lap.

"I called Glen to tell him about Tiffany," Mignon said sheepishly.

"Friday's my day off," Glen said giving me his teeth-whitened smile.

"He's going to babysit with Tiffany while I run to the store to get her some things."

"Uh huh. Well, I'd better get going." I held my laughter until I was out the door.

I raced home, nearly losing my balance on the snow-filled sidewalks. No blinking light. Jory had taken me at my word that I'd be busy. Perhaps it was good. Maybe I needed time to slow down. Maybe Jory had been my diversion from the horribleness around me, but I hoped not. Still, I hadn't been walking around paralyzed with fear like I might have been if he hadn't been lighting ever possible fire in my body.

I changed the sheets in the guest room that had not too many days before been the scene of the best lovemaking I'd engaged in. Suzi and I shared everything, but I wouldn't tell her about Jory, not yet. She'd think I'd committed another impulsive act—like my whole freshman year at Michigan. "But you don't even know him," she'd said over and over to me.

Then I made myself a squishy white bread turkey sandwich. I also nuked some stuffing. I had enough food to feed a family for a week. Hannibal's battle of the bourbon balls, causing my company's smaller-than-usual appetite, had seen to that.

After I picked up the house and turned the fire on in the den, I pulled out my laptop. I'd do some writing while I waited for Suzi. Where had I left Harriet?

Howler let out a sigh and settled in for a nap by the fire.

Though my world in Camphor had taken on a sinister twist, Harriet's had become even darker and more threatening. Besides the swirling dangers surrounding her, she lived alone and had a hateful family.

She was late closing at the bank so Harriet knew it was fast food time. She stopped at the deli to pick up a Reuben salad and a bottle of raspberry cherry soda. It was her intent to read her Oprah Book Club book and get to bed early. The next day was Saturday, and if she was very lucky none of her family would intrude.

As soon as she reached her clapboard house at the end of town, she knew something was wrong. She wished she'd let that nice Scrap Sloane walk her home. He was the only man with whom she'd felt comfortable in a long time, and he was handsome in a rugged sort of way. Still, Harriet was dubbed the family spinster, and she didn't see how she could turn into someone who challenged their opinion of her.

It was especially dark outside and her motion detector needed a bulb. She could barely see to put the key in the door. When she stepped inside, a foul smell greeted her. Something was decaying. Later she wouldn't be able to tell how she knew it, but at that moment she knew death was in the next room.

I loved the story. For the next few hours, Harriet and more dead bodies captivated me, pushing Jory and my own fearful existence totally out of my mind. The grandfather clock told me it was nine pm. Where was Suzi? She should be here by now. I checked the machine to see if I'd missed a message. Nothing.

I tried Suzi several times on her cell, but got the same cheery, "Please leave your name and number, and I'll get back to you as soon as I can" message.

By ten o'clock, I had gone into warp panic and called her home, which meant I'd have to find a way to talk to her insufferable husband. No answer there. I'd never forgive myself if something happened to Suzi when she was on her way to help me.

I started looking through my address book for other people who might know how to contact Suzi. Her parents were both dead and besides her husband Aaron, I knew very little about Suzi's life in the city. My hands shook as I rifled through the pages. No names jumped out that connected to Suzi and her Chicago world.

The doorbell startled me and woke Howler, asleep at my feet. Standing in the doorway was a mussed up Suzi. Her usually lustrous black hair hung limply on her shoulders, and her eyes looked sunken. She reminded me of the way we looked in college when we pulled all-nighters during finals.

"Where have you been?" I hugged her and pulled her into the house at the same time. "I've been so worried."

"I tried to call. My phone needs charging, and I stopped at a gas station, but their phone didn't work. The employees looked a little scary so I got out of there. Then I had a flat tire. What a nightmare!"

"Oh poor baby!" I was rushing around making a turkey sandwich and hot chocolate. "You look so tired. I tried to call Aaron."

"We're not together right now. We'll be fine, and I'm not here to talk about my problems. We're just going through a rough patch. It is so great to see you— and all in one piece, too. What the hell is going on here?"

"Don't I wish I knew." I quickly catalogued what I could tell Suzi and what I should leave until after the murders had been solved. I didn't want to scare her to death. I put the sandwich, hot chocolate and a piece of apple pie in front of her. "You probably know just about as much as I do except that a friend of mine was just attacked, not killed but nearly frightened to death."

"E! This is worse than Chicago. I don't think there's ever been a murder in my neighborhood, which is a whole lot bigger than this place. Little Camphor with a crime wave. Imagine that!"

Suzi and I tried to stay awake to talk, but within an hour, she was sleeping soundly in the guest room. An hour or so later, after I'd started the new David Rosenfelt book and decided that a mystery, no matter how funny and suspenseful, might not be my best bet for before-bed reading, I, too, was sound asleep.

It was still dark when I woke, startled by a noise that seemed to come from outside, just outside my bedroom. For a few seconds, I couldn't move. It was as if someone was scaling the side of the house. Electric currents pulsed through me. Howler scooted closer and buried his head in my covers. I listened for sounds from Suzi's room. Silence. I lay there debating if I should get up or just wait to see what happened next. My mouth was dry and my face ached. I needed to take a breath. I needed to get some courage! I pushed Howler aside, stealthily put on slippers and a robe and slowly walked toward the window. At first I heard nothing. Then something seemed to scrape the side of the house. Next a thud.

"Shhhhh." I warned Howler when he began his own guttural, fear driven growl. Still no noise from Suzi's room.

Outside I heard another thump. I edged toward the dresser, retrieved my phone, and dialed what I hoped was 911. In the dark it was hard to tell. "Michigan State Police," said a voice.

"I think someone is breaking into my house." I whispered, trying to hear both the voice on the phone and whatever might be going on outside. "Can you come quickly?"

"Your address?" The voice was disinterested. The person had done this a lot.

The moment I said I lived in Camphor, however, the voice came alive, telling me to lock my door, stay in my room, and listen for the police. "I'll stay on until they get there. Don't leave your bedroom." It commanded.

"I'll stay here, but . . ." I was cut off by sounds from outside.

"Hey!" a voice shouted right below my window. I waited seconds before I crept over to look out. Two figures ran away from the house, one in front of the other. My heart broke when I recognized the second figure as Jory. He'd broken into my house! As the voice on the phone asked again and again if I were still there, I couldn't speak. My heart was shattered. My worst fears were confirmed. Jory was connected in awful and undeniable ways to the murders that were swallowing Camphor. I remained frozen until the lights and sirens pulled into my yard.

Chapter Twelve

Javier, with his arm in a sling, was the officer who investigated the break-in. "There was more than one person," he said, confirming what I already knew. "Did you see anything?"

Right then was when I should have told him about seeing Jory, about believing that the man I had fallen head over heels for just a few weeks earlier was connected to all that had terrified Camphor. Instead I shook my head and spent the next several hours figuring out why. The only rational reason I could arrive at was that Jory was his brother-in-law. What if Javier was involved, too?

"E! What's happened?" Suzi, groggy and confused, appeared in the kitchen while I was still talking to Javier.

"People broke into the house. The police are investigating."

"They broke in while we were here—while we were sleeping?! Oh, my god! E! This is terrible." Her hands shook as she poured a cup of cold coffee. "Did you catch them?" she asked Javier without waiting to be introduced—not necessary under the circumstances.

"No, but we will." Javier said. "Maybe you should try to go back to bed." He said to both of us. "I'll post a man outside. And I think I'm going to sleep right here on your couch. If I don't, Jory will never forgive me."

"Who's Jory?" Suzi asked.

I didn't respond.

I should tell Javier. I knew that. And I knew there was little chance that Javier was involved in the murders. Maybe I harbored a smidge of hope that Jory would have plausible denial, that he just happened by. Maybe I also believed the moon was made of green cheese. I'd have to tell Javier—later. I'd let it be up to him to deal with Lucy—and Mama Esqueda.

I fell into bed sure that I wouldn't be able to sleep, but sunlight was streaming through the windows by the time I awoke. Outside the policeman was still there. Small comfort when the image of Jory running across the lawn was stamped in my mind.

Javier was gone. And there was no noise from Suzi's room. I put my head in my pillow and dissolved into tears. I guess heartbreak trumps panic. I couldn't sleep.

I let Howler into the backyard. At least he was happy, lying in the sunny snow for quite a while before he ambled back in to get breakfast. I dumped out the cold, stale coffee and started a new pot of my favorite hazelnut cream. Someone opened the front door, scaring me to death.

"Suzi! I thought you were still in bed!"

"I took a walk. I've been up since the crack of dawn. I don't know when I've been as scared as I am here. E, you need to come home with me until this is settled. Let's go now. I'll grab my stuff, and you pack a few things." The dark circles that had been under her eyes when she arrived were even more pronounced, and I noticed a bruise on her wrist. I didn't have a chance to question it though. She turned to me, "You seem to be taking this all very well. Don't you realize that it's as if this town is under siege?"

"Suzi, I've been living with this—we all have—for weeks. Try not to think about it. You know me; if I think about it, I'll have a panic attack so great that I'll never come out of it. Now sit down and let me feed you breakfast."

"Wow!" she said pulling her hat off her headscarf and releasing her ink black hair. She stared at the concoction I was putting together in a saucepan. "That looks yummy."

"See? I know a thing or two about the kitchen. I'll make Paula Deen's wonderful hot chocolate, I brought the fixings, and we'll talk. Oh did I tell you that the recipe is made with sweetened condensed milk? Enough said."

"This is orgasmic!" Suzi grabbed for a napkin to wipe a layer of chocolate from her mouth. "Great idea. We need this."

"Well," I said, "I know why I need this wonderful treat, but I'm not sure about you. You look tired, and that's a bruise on your wrist. Talk!" The roles were reversed, ever since my panic attacks staked their claim on me my first year at Michigan, Suzi had looked after me and my embarrassing neuroses.

"I needed to get out of town." She set down the still steaming mug. "Get that look off your face. It's mostly work, and once I get some rest everything will be fine. Now tell me what's been going on here. I've been so scared for you. Little Goody Two Shoes Camphor has been all over the Chicago stations. What's wrong that no one can find a murderer in a town of about ten people?"

"I'm ashamed to admit that you probably know about as much as I do." I wasn't convinced that what made Suzi look so stressed and tired was business. "The worst part is what it's doing to the town. We all look at each other with suspicion. Madge and Mignon are nutcases at varying times—then sometimes I'm nuttier than anyone." I thought of my fools-rush-in style romance with Jory.

"Oh tell me about Mignon and Madge. I hope I'm in half as good shape as they are when I'm their age. They are so dear."

"Not so dear lately. They're engaging in the battle of the dogs." I told her about Hannibal and Tiffany.

"Oh I needed this!" Suzi said laughing so hard she had to work to catch her breath. "Those two should sell tickets!"

"It's worse now." She had me laughing too. "Oh no, I just remembered that Mignon wants to take us to dinner tonight."

"Oh let's. She'll keep our mind off anything serious and real."

"Right. Serious and real is seldom Mignon or Madge's focus. Oh, and you should hear them complain that their hairdresser had the nerve to take a month off for her hysterectomy. Didn't she realize how important it was for them to have their hair looking good for the winter formal at the country club?"

"Madge has someone do her hair? I thought it looked that way because she didn't get it done professionally."

We laughed as we did when we were undergrads, and it felt absolutely wonderful to be so silly and wacky. For at least a few minutes there was no thought of murders—and no thought of Jory, John, or any other of life's complications.

"I know murder has put the damper on my life, but I think it's more than work that has you looking so tired." I stopped laughing and zeroed in on the issue that plagued me since I saw Suzi in my doorway. Exactly why did she look so worn out?

"Well, since you won't let it go, and since at some time today I would like to get out and do something, I'll tell you that Aaron and I are having a little trouble. I know it's just because we've been working too hard and had practically no time for each other. But I swear that sometimes I don't know him at all."

Or you do, I thought but didn't say. "Let's have another cup of this sinfully rich hot chocolate and you tell me all about what's been going on. And when we get tired of this, we can go to the hard stuff." I pointed toward the Hazelnut lattes.

For over an hour Suzi and I filled each other in about our lives. It sounded to me that Aaron had become an even bigger creep than I remembered. I told Suzi a bit about Jory but just a bit.

"He sounds too good to be true."

"He may be. I'm almost afraid that he could be. I'm too busy right now for a man in my life. We're taking a hiatus. Then we'll see."

"Is John part of your hesitancy?"

"Not at all. That's over."

"I hope so. You never seemed in love with him. And love is never to be underestimated in a relationship," she said ruefully.

"Oh and I'm actually at page fifty-five of a book." Time to change the subject.

"You got past page fifty?" she high-fived me. "I never doubted that you would one day make zillions writing books. You are such a born writer. Not that there's anything wrong with your day job," she added, aware that I am more than sensitive to criticism regarding my under-appreciated vocation. "Tell me about your book."

"It's not literary—not the kind of writing that would make Professor Combs proud. But I love it. I have this character who has found herself smack in the middle of death and destruction. Don't tell anyone, but she's based on many people in Camphor."

"Imagine that!"

"Right," I laughed. "Harriet—she's my central character—is brave and curious and a real risk taker. Not a carbon copy of me."

"How are the panic attacks?" she asked.

"There. Sometimes they're worse than others. You know, though, I haven't had a full blown one since the murders started."

"You've always been better in an emergency than in a sea of calm. It's like you live for catastrophes."

"I hope that's not true. It probably is, though."

"Anyway, I've missed you and brought this great pizza. I sneaked it into your freezer last night. If we're going out for dinner, how about if you and I very sinfully indulge in it for lunch?"

"Good idea." I knew that my jeans would be once again feeling too tight and that Suzi with her perpetually waiflike look wouldn't add an ounce.

"And I have an idea about your book. One of my neighbors works for a publisher. Finish it and I'll show it to Eugenie, ok?"

"I haven't even thought about publishing it, but just knowing that it might be a possibility has me excited. Thanks, roomy."

We were each on our third piece of the best pizza I'd ever had when someone rang the bell. It was Jory. For the first time since I'd met him, I wasn't glad to see him.

"I know you have company," he said looking swarthy and appealing, "but I wanted to make sure you're ok."

"I'm fine." I said, chills all over my body, and this time they had nothing to do with Jory's Fahrenheit Scale sex appeal. I wanted him to go away closer, but if you can't trust someone then you can't love someone, can you? "Come in and meet my roommate Suzi," I said filling an enormously awkward space. "Suzi, this is my friend Jory Esqueda. Jory, my college roommate Suzi." I could tell from the smile on Suzi's face that she thought I'd struck the mother load.

"It's nice to meet you. E will have to bring you to Chicago sometime." She gave me a quick wink, which I'm sure Jory noticed.

"We'll have to do that," Jory said. "E, could we talk for a minute?"

I didn't want to, but to keep Suzi from asking questions to which I had no answer, I followed Jory out to my back steps, pulling the door closed behind us.

"What's up?" I tried to sound chipper, but I sounded phony.

"That's what I want to know. You seem distant. Is everything all right?"

"I guess. Jory, I think we've rushed things. I need to slow down and think."

I felt sick saying it and he looked sick hearing it. Then he was angry.

"Is it Kidston? Never mind. I think I know the answer. Well, give me a call if you change your mind."

He was gone and I was dizzy. What had I done?

"Now that is much more like it." Suzi said when I returned to the kitchen. "E, he is adorable and charming and sexy. Who knew that someone like Jory Esqueda would be right in your backyard?"

"I think it's over—not that it ever really got off the ground. I don't think I'm ready, and I think he's not telling me the complete truth about a lot of things."

"You're a big girl," she took a fourth piece of pizza, "but before you do something you can't undo, really think about it. He is really a doll, E, but if he's someone you can't trust, lose him now. Believe me, I know. But damn he's darling!

"Well, looks aren't everything," I said taking another piece of pizza, which would do much more damage on my hips than on Suzi's. "I want to pick up a bottle of wine and drop it off at a friend's who is recovering from a beating. It will only take a minute. Want to come?"

"Oh god. On top of everything else, you have a friend who was beaten? Is there another awful thing you're hiding from me?"

"Later."

Suzi drove and the elegance of her special edition BMW made me think it might be time to turn the trusty Toyota in for a sleeker model. The drive in her car was smooth and not a creak did I hear.

"Stop here." I pointed to Bacchanalia. "I'll only be a minute."

The man inside the upscale wine store knew immediately which rich red wine Maurice favored. "You're about the tenth person to come in here and get him something." He said as he artfully put a bow around my bottle. "In fact, even Mr. Brunson was in here buying himself a bunch of wine. That was before his accident though. He said he thought he would be laid up a while. Guess he was planning on having more plastic surgery. "The clerk sounded snarly, like one of Maurice's jilted boy toys, which he probably was. Maurice had lots of friends.

"Thanks for waiting," I said to Suzi who had been resting her head against the headrest. "Are you feeling all right?"

"I'm just tired. It's so good to be here, though."

Her phone had fallen on my seat so when it rang, I started to hand it to her. "I think it's Aaron," I said as I studied the CID.

"I'll call him later." Her expression was a combination of anger and disgust—totally foreign to the Suzi I knew and loved.

"Are you going to tell me what's going on?" I asked. "What's really going on with you and Aaron?"

"Just married people stuff. We're fine." She forced a smile. "You'll have to tell me where we're going."

"Back to Cinnamon Street. Maurice lives at the far end, the rich end." I signaled for her to turn in order to get back to our street. I noticed that John's car was parked in front of his office and that Whitey's police car was in front of the Camphor Police Station. Harvey had been buried and our little town was still alive and well. Well, most of it was alive.

"Come on in and meet Maurice." I said

"Maybe he's not up for meeting new people." Suzi said.

"If he's not, Martha will let us know—Martha's his housekeeper."

Martha ushered us right into the den where Maurice was having his nails manicured.

"Oh E, darling," he smiled broadly. "I am so glad you are here. I have been dying from lack of gossip. This is Mitch, my hairdresser. He's been good enough to help me get these nails in order." He flashed a well-cared for hand replete with clear nail polish. "And who is your stunningly beautiful friend?"

Even Mitch looked up to greet Suzi who always turns a significant number of heads. "This is my college roommate Suzi—from Chicago. Remember that I visit her there?"

"Ah yes, our little girl in the big city," Maurice laughed and grabbed his side. "Oh I can't do that."

"Now tell us what happened," I said sitting on the hassock in front of his chair. Suzi sat in an adjacent chair.

"Why it was just the most unimaginable horror." He said calling on all his dramatic skills. "I was out having dinner with friends. When I got home, I put the key in the door, opened it and was flung to the floor, flung viciously and violently." He leaned back to take a breath as he recounted his trauma.

"Oh you are so lucky you weren't killed." I hated the thought of Camphor without the colorful Maurice.

"I, too, think about how close I came to being killed." Maurice's eyes filled. "I have only been kind to people," he said in his best diva tone. "I couldn't imagine why someone would do such a thing. Glen said I was extremely lucky. I have some badly bruised ribs and a sore knee, but it could have been so much worse."

"Thank god it wasn't." I took both his hands in mine. "We brought a few things to help your recovery." I retrieved the bottle of wine I'd left on the table when we entered the room. "The man at the wine shop seemed to know you and said you would like this."

"That's Giovanni," Maurice said as he admired the wine. "He would indeed know what I like."

"Well, we're going out to dinner with Mignon. We'd better get going. Oh, did you hear she got a dog?" I said as Suzi and I rose to leave.

"Mignon with a dog? I never thought she would allow anything that breathes into that treasured house of hers. A dog? How big a dog?"

"Not big—kind of a teaspoonful of a dog, but darling. You'll have to see her when you're well."

"Maybe," he said.

And maybe not, I thought. Maurice and Mignon would never renew the friendship of their youth.

"Are you afraid?" Suzi said on the way home.

"I'm always afraid. You know that," I said. "But this time I am afraid for all of us, not just me. My greatest fear is that one of the ladies will get in trouble, and I will be too knee-knocking panicked to help them."

"You're braver than you know," Suzi said as we pulled into my driveway. "I can't believe it," she added. "I'm hungry again."

"You're not alone," I laughed unlocking the house and taking a minute to make sure the only strange noise I heard was Howler's feet clinking on the hardwood floors as he sauntered up to greet us.

One problem with joining Mignon at the club was that I wouldn't be able to have a private talk with Suzi. I needed more girl-talk time. Another problem was that the club was ritzy, which meant dressy. Suzi, always prepared, had a darling short beige, strapless cocktail dress and brown shawl that made her even more beautiful. I dragged out my one and only little black dress, black nylons, and black shrug that made me passable but not "W" worthy. I noticed when I pulled on my nylons that I had some paint from the Kidstons' dining room still on the back of my leg. I made a mental note to shower more carefully.

We picked up Mignon who looked trend-setting elegant in black silk and fur. The surprise was that Tiffany was also in a little black fur coat.

"Oh she is as cute as E said," Suzi gushed, as Mignon sparkled with pride.

"Pull out very slowly with your lights off," Mignon said as we helped her into Suzi's car. "I didn't invite you-know-who."

"Look at the bay window," I pointed to the house next door. "You-know-who sees us."

"Serves her right. I might have invited her if she hadn't been so rude when she was over this afternoon. She had the audacity to say she couldn't tell who was more beautiful Tiffany or that horror she calls a dog. Can you imagine? Then she said—dead seriously—that I should make sure Tiffany didn't get flushed down the toilet. As if I can't watch my own dog! But the worst thing was when she said she was sure Tiffany isn't a pedigreed dog, that her bottom teeth are crooked. Imagine! She owns the hound from hell and she's making cracks about my wovely wittle woofy."

"I'm sure she didn't mean it that way," I said, knowing Madge well enough to know that that was exactly how she meant it. "She doesn't like the club anyway."

"It's because they turned her down," Mignon was placing Tiffany in a large fur bag. "You know that. It was after Cissy died and she and Duane inherited her wad of money. Duane wanted to join the club. They turned them down. I want you to know that I voted for them, fought to let them in, in fact. I never told Madge that. Your mother talked a bunch of us into voting them in. However, someone else led a campaign against them. You'll never believe who it was."

"Who?" I asked, surprised I'd not heard the story before.

"Maurice. That was the last straw for me with him."

"Maurice. I find that hard to believe." Blackballing Madge seemed far from Maurice's egalitarian nature.

"He's a real snob, you know. His mother was a diabolical piece of work who got a job as the housekeeper as soon as Homer Brunson's wife was killed in that plane crash in the Canary Islands. Homer was Horace's younger brother and a lesser heir to the Brunson billions. Anyway, Maurice's mother chased poor Homer until she shamelessly caught him. Maurice came six months after the marriage. But Maurice still acts as if he speaks but to God."

"I guess." I still wasn't sure about Mignon's account of why Madge didn't get into the country club. Maurice and Mignon didn't get along so maybe she was pinning something on him that wasn't his fault.

The country club is one of my guilty pleasures. Once my mother died, I dropped the family membership because I couldn't see myself splurging on such an extravagance as the twenty thousand dollar annual fee. I did love to go as Mignon's guest though. It is posh to the hilt, all velvet and dark, expensive wood. The pictures are museum worthy and the staff treats you like royalty. I'm kind of a reverse snob: I wouldn't for the life of me join the club, but I feel great when I eat a meal or attend a party there—once in a while.

"This is as fabulous as I remember," Suzi whispered. "Talk about old money. There's not a place in Chicago that can rival it. Remember the fun we had when your mother would bring us here?"

"That was fun. She would insist that we order three desserts and everyone shared everyone else's. We usually went home with our faces aching from laughing and our stomachs aching from over-eating."

"Oh that darling mother of yours." Mignon touched my hand. "Do you have any idea how grateful I am you are so much like her?"

"Oh yes," I laughed, "tiny and poised."

"No," Mignon said even more seriously. "You are kind and gentle and thoughtful. You make my old age manageable."

"It's hard to see you as old, Mrs. Dalton," Suzi said. "You have such beautiful skin, and you don't ever look a day older than the last time I saw you."

"Well, just for that," Mignon perked up, "I think we are going to order everything rich and decadent on the menu, and then we'll have three desserts! We'll start with the elephant garlic spread and crab cakes."

"Count me in," I had picked up my menu to begin studying the tantalizing dishes when Suzi softly said, "My! My! Look who's here."

The three of us looked across the room to see John and Caroline Kidston enter with another couple. I recognized the man as Gray Damron, one of John's fraternity brothers.

My instinct was to ignore them and return to studying the menu. John's smile made that impossible. The four of them headed toward our table.

"Mrs. Dalton, E and Suzi, it's great to see you." John was graciousness and gentility personified.

"E Clare! It's been a decade." Gray Damron came over to give my shoulders a squeeze. His very sweet-looking and pleasantly round wife seemed like someone I would like. Caroline Kidston, gorgeous in a long emerald green couture gown and diamonds was someone I would never like. She smiled a smile that never wavered in its determination to remain despite the hatred that filled her eyes.

"Mignon is treating us to dinner," I said, exhibiting my usual no-gift for gab.

"We belong," snapped Caroline sending a ripple of discomfort through the people in her group. "And we had better head for our table. I see the maître d' waiting for us." She led and the rest followed. "See you Monday. E is painting my nursery," she said to the nice-looking woman as they left. "Oh, there's daddy," she ran over to a distinguished, slightly tipsy older man who entered from the opposite side of the room.

"Great to see you all," John's eyes rested on me. "I was in town for a conference last spring, Suzi, and I thought about looking you up. Got too busy so it didn't happen." John's smile was sincere and perfect.

"John is such a good guy," Suzi said as soon as John returned to his table. "I can't say I've ever liked his wife, though." I could tell she was waiting for my reaction. Mignon saved me.

"His reptile, you mean," Mignon petted Tiffany who was sitting patiently in the bag next to her. "With all the people getting whacked away at in town, it's a pity someone doesn't take an axe to her."

"Mignon! Don't say that!" I couldn't believe my ears.

"I didn't mean it." She said with not a bit of credibility. "That's nothing to joke about is it? She is a pain in the arse though."

Considering what was going on in Camphor, I hated to say that we had a meal to die for, but we did. The prime rib that I had was soft-butter consistency and perfectly seasoned. Suzi had the lobster and that, too, was beyond wonderful. Mignon had chosen phyllo and herb encrusted salmon which she shared and which was also five-star excellent. The house salad full of fresh lettuces and fruits with a poppy seed dressing complemented everything else perfectly..

"I will not take no for an answer," Mignon said as she directed us to order a surfeit of desserts: several varieties of cheesecake, tiramisu and chocolate cake. As we waited for our over-the-top treats, I stole glances toward the Kidston party. All eyes were on Caroline who was talking and talking and talking. John was tapping his fingers on the table. Poor John.

When we got to Mignon's, I walked her and Tiffany inside. "Thanks so much," I said to her. "It was so nice of you to include Suzi."

"She's family, too," said Mignon. We both looked at the house next door. The lights were all out, and a head was no longer peering out the window. "Maybe we'll take Madge next week if you're up for it. She is NOT taking Hannibal, though."

I smiled on the way back to the car thinking that Mignon cared much more about her neighbor and friend than she let on. I also took note that for the first time, she had referred to Hannibal by his name. As I turned the key in the ignition, I thought about how handsome John looked and how much shared background might matter. Was my mother right? Would John have been perfect for me? If so, why did I go weak whenever I was within a mile of Jory Esqueda? Turns out that panic and arousal have similar symptoms. But I could control panic much more easily.

Chapter Thirteen

Suzi was up and doing some work on her computer by the time I had showered.

"I put Howler outside," she said. "I have only a few things to do and then we can pour ourselves lots of coffee and talk." She went back to emailing.

"In honor of your visit, I am going to use the pricey espresso machine the ladies gave me."

"Sounds good," she said totally involved in what she was doing.

I read the directions to refresh my memory and then brewed us up vanilla almond lattes. Suzi was still working as I handed a steamy cup to her. I then pulled out my own computer and returned to Harriet's story. Again, time and my fingers flew as the bodies and suspects mounted in Harriet's life.

"Is that your story?" Suzi was reading over my shoulder. "Print off some pages and let me read."

"OK." I was hesitant to let anyone into Harriet's and my story. "Let's not talk about it, though. I don't want my momentum to die down."

"Sure." She took some pages from me, walked to the sofa where she lay down, resting her legs over the edge.

I returned to making the lattes. While Suzi read, I checked my email. There was nothing from Suzi, my most constant correspondent, because she was right next to me in the den. Steve Overton had let me know that Caroline Kidston had contacted him about the paint in the baby's room because Pru's hadn't the shade of blue she wanted. Thank you. Thank you. No more spreading peanut butter. Steve also told me the paint would be in early Monday so I wouldn't be behind schedule.

Next was a message from Earlene reiterating that Mignon was off the hook on Horace's murder, and asking if I could meet at her office a little after five on Monday.

The last message had a sender I didn't know, and usually I leave those totally alone, but the subject heading "Murder" got me. I hit the pad before I had time to think about it.

You are not paying attention, E,

I have tried and tried to tell you that you need to stay away from danger.

Instead, you run toward it.

I fear I must give you what you want. Death is at your door.

I slammed the computer shut causing Suzi to look up.

"You ok?"

"Fine. I'm just tired of work. I'm going to see if I have any mail and then I'm going to order you to shut your computer so we can talk."

"You're shaking."

"It's just that free-floating anxiety thing," I said.

"What about medicine, E? This has been going on for a long time."

"I'll be fine. I have Xanax but take it only when I absolutely have to."

I opened the door to get my mail and tripped over a slaughtered deer. I passed out with Suzi shouting "E!" as I went down.

I was out for a matter of seconds and regained consciousness with Suzi madly dialing her cell phone. "Is this the state police?" she asked into the sliver of a phone.

"No!" I shouted as I pulled myself up. "Hang up."

She dropped the phone. "Why? You need help."

"I think you're right," I said glad that nothing hurt or throbbed. "I promise to go get some little white pills from Dr. Newell tomorrow. Right now I know who to call."

"Ok, but you do remember that there is a deer carcass in your doorway, right?"

"I remember." I looked through the white pages for Javier Rodriguez's name. There was an L. and since I knew that policemen don't like to let people know where they live, I thought maybe he'd listed the phone under Lucy's name. The television news report said that Javier was back at work so I didn't feel guilty giving him a call.

"Javier. This is E Clary. Remember me? Good. Well, I think there's something going on over here that you need to know about. Could you come over sometime? Fifteen minutes—sure. That would be great."

I hung up the phone and went back to Suzi, standing with her arms across her chest and no smile, "What in the hell is going on here? I'm taking you back to Chicago when I leave this afternoon."

"I'm as confused as you, but I know I'll be fine. You know me, I always panic at the slightest hint of change. And a dead deer on my doorstep is a big change." I laughed. Suzi didn't.

"I'm going to call work and stay another day. There's nothing I'm doing there tomorrow that I can't just as well do here."

"I hate to have you change your schedule just for me. "In truth, I was relieved that she might hang around a bit more.

"Like I said, there's nothing for me to go back to."

"What about Aaron?" I sat down on a kitchen chair and she sat opposite me. "How about if we talk about why you really came here?"

"I told you. I was worried about you."

"Uh uh. I'm not buying it. You've been here over twenty four hours, and from what I've seen you've never once called Aaron."

"Boy, there's no hiding anything from you, Sherlock," she said. "I've asked Aaron for a legal separation. There have been problems for a long, long time. He's into this day trading thing and has been spending a lot of time out of the country."

"What about his job at the law firm?" I'd be the last person to criticize someone for the job they did, but from what I remembered Aaron had a great job.

"He says he can make more money doing what he's doing, but he's always so stressed and gets mad at the drop of a hat. I can't take it anymore."

"Why does he have to be out of the country?" I asked.

"Why indeed. I've asked him and he says the work he does requires it. I think he's into drugs a bit, using them that is. And, E, there are women. They call at all hours and he pretends it's business but I can tell by the way he talks to them when he leaves the room, it's not business. I'm terrified that Aaron has gotten himself into something, and I think it's something dangerous. When I confront him, he tells me I'm crazy. Finally, the last time I tried to get him to talk, he walked out."

"God, Suzi, and to think I've been so wrapped up in what's going on here that I've hardly paid attention to you. Some friend I am."

"About two months ago I started getting these calls where someone would call and then hang up when I answered. I asked Aaron about it, and he said that it was nothing. Well, the first thing that came to my mind was another woman so one night I let him answer the phone, and I picked up one in the office. It was a man and he said something like, 'I'm tired of waiting. You either clean up this mess or I will.' E, the voice made the hair on my arms stand up."

"You have to go to the police." My fingers and toes were tingling at the thought of the danger Suzi might be in. "There's Javier pulling into the driveway. He'll know what to do."

"Don't tell him," her fingers dug into my arm. "Aaron told me that he knows what he's doing and that he'll be ok very shortly. He said that if I go to the authorities, I could get him killed."

"I won't tell him why, but I'll ask Javier for a law enforcement officer that he knows and trusts in Chicago."

"You do and I will never speak to you again." Her jaw was set and her eyes deadly serious. "I told you this in secret."

"OK," I said reluctantly as I opened the door. "Javier, I'm so sorry to have to get you out of your house. First, how are you feeling?" He looked pretty good except for the bruises on the left side of his face and his bandaged left hand.

"No problem. I'm fine. I was just having a beer with Jory. Wow! Someone really got to this guy—wasn't a car. I can tell you that." Javier studied the unfortunate deer. "Was there a note or anything?"

"Just the deer." I looked past Javier to see Jory sitting in his police car. I hated myself for thinking it, but Javier provided a perfect cover if Jory was behind the death and fear in Camphor.

"Jory and I were watching football." Javier nodded in Jory's direction.

"He's welcome to come in," I said.

"He already said he can't tonight. Hey, you guys having trouble or something? He's been in one terrible mood." Javier didn't explain but walked in my house, pulled a note pad from his jacket along with a pencil and started making notes. "This whole thing has me frickin' frustrated. Why is someone coming back to you again and again. Maybe it's about the missing files."

"Files?" I asked.

"The files that John Kidston and I found were incomplete. When we looked in the file drawer, files from the early sixties were missing. It was obvious that there was a gap. We'll talk to you about that later."

"Do you have any idea about who the guilty party is?" I asked apprehensively.

"Not really. That's what's frustrating everyone. I feel it's someone right under our noses."

Or sitting in your car, I thought.

"We're combing through the files, though, to see if there's something we've missed."

"I can't help feeling that it's tied into Brunson Spice," I said. "The name Brunson comes up over and over. The files you took covered the years from the late 1950's to the early seventies. Maybe if you look at what went on at Brunson Spice during those years, you'll get an answer."

"That's our hope," he said. "Man, this is so damn frustrating!" he slammed the pad into his jacket pocket. "Can you tolerate this thing being here until later this afternoon? I can get someone over here by 3."

"It's fine. We'll just go out the back door." I laughed, trying to lighten the atmosphere, but Javier didn't seem to see the humor.

"I'm going to have a police car stationed on this street at night. If you see or hear anything at all that's odd or out of place, let the officer on duty know, ok?"

"Ok."

I walked Javier to the car and smiled at Jory who nodded and then returned to whatever he was working on. It was over—whatever it was that we'd had. I couldn't look at him without doubting him, and now he couldn't look at me. I walked back to the house with a massive sense of loss.

Suzi's suitcase was in the hallway. "I had better get home." She said pulling her car keys from her purse. "I'm so glad that you're going to have someone posted outside the house. I feel better now."

"But I don't feel better. I don't want you to be mad at me. I just really think that whatever Aaron is involved in could impact you in a dangerous way. Don't be angry with me, OK? I just love you like a sister."

"Oh, E," she hugged me, "I'm not angry at you. I'm mad at myself. How could I have been so stupid not to question him much sooner?"

"Stay here. You can call work and take some days off," I said. "Or I'll call for you and tell them that you've contracted an as yet unidentified, highly contagious disease."

Her face broke into her beautiful smile for the first time that morning. "You don't have to do that. I'm not in danger—not like you. And Aaron and I will either make it or we won't. Now you take care of yourself. I'll call you when I get home, ok?"

"Ok." I watched her pull away from the house with a sense of dread. If she didn't call me in three hours to tell me she was home, I'd call her.

I let Howler out back, thinking that my days of walking him were over until they found out who was raising Cain in Camphor. I also wasn't going to let Howler see what was on my porch. There was probably a bit of hunting dog in him somewhere. While he was out eating the new fallen snow, I pulled out the laptop and resumed Harriet's story, page sixty-eight. It turns out the very self-sufficient Harriet couldn't help being drawn to Scrap Sloan, but he had a dark, threatening past.

I let myself fall into the lovemaking scene I created between Harriet and her man of mystery. My writing was unencumbered by the deer's body, the many corpses, and Suzi's problems. Harriet and the man in her bed took me to page eighty before I knew it. Only when she called him Jory instead of Scrap did I realize how much I missed those dark eyes and possessive touches.

I left Harriet with a knife to her throat and a hooded man's man hot breath whispering threats. It woke me from my Jory daydreams. If I couldn't trust Jory, I couldn't love Jory.

Sunday evenings are usually my night to get ready for work and take a leisurely bath. Because of all that had gone on that day, though, I jumped at Madge's invitation to join Hannibal and her for her special taco salad. Madge, certainly no Julia Childs in the kitchen, made a mean taco salad. I had tons of food in my fridge but didn't want to eat or be alone.

Hannibal's looks had not improved. It was obvious that Madge was trying to bring some semblance of beauty to him, but his big gawky self looked even more absurd with the enormous pink polka dot bow she'd put on his unruly mop. "Doesn't he look just like a kewpie doll?" she smiled. "He's really beautiful in his own way, don't you think?" She was dishing up an enormous amount of her mixture of taco seasoned ground beef, tomatoes, onions, black olives, and Doritos with her own special sauce for flavoring.

"He's such a special dog." I petted him, and he pushed against me for more. "I think he's a lucky dog to have you."

"He is," she smiled. "The trainer says he's very smart. Oh, E, it's just the most fun thing to have this dog to think about instead of all the awful, bloody things that are going on around us. Until Hannibal came into my life, I had no idea how desperate I was feeling."

"I'm sure Hannibal feels the same way about you." I started to throw Hannibal a taco-flavored Dorito, but thought better of it when I remembered the dance of the bourbon balls.

"What do you think about that little thing Mignon has? You think she'd be ashamed to try to pass it off as a dog. Anything that poops Tootsie Rolls is not a dog!"

I laughed, not quite following her logic. However, I did know that the question created a potential mine field. The ladies had become as competitive about their dogs as they were about their gardens. If I let either of them think I liked one dog better than the other, I was in deep dooky, and it would be stuff that I, not the dogs, made.

"Vi Thornton is over there tonight." Madge pointed in the direction of Mignon's. She's back here for the board meeting tomorrow. I guess they have to decide what's going to happen to Brunson Spice."

"Mignon says you'll be part of that decision."

"Yeah," Madge laughed. "Whoever would have thunk it! Cissy Weatherbee sure changed our lives. Except of course, Duane isn't here to enjoy it." She wiped her eyes. "Or maybe he is. Don't tell that nose for news next door, but sometimes I think that Hannibal is really Duane come back to guard me—kind of like my guardian angel-dog. Do you think that's possible?"

"Well, anything is possible." I took another bite of the best taco salad anyone has ever had and hoped that Madge wasn't wandering away from odd to just plain crazy.

"Didn't you hear us knocking?" Mignon and her cousin Vi walked in from the direction of the kitchen. "We must have pounded for five minutes, right Vi?"

"Well, five minutes may be a bit of an exaggeration," Vi was petite and perfect in a forest green warm up tight enough to display breasts that gave new meaning to the term Silicon Valley. "E, dear, are you still seeing that positively mouth-watering man you were with the last time we met? Gorgeous doesn't begin to describe him."

"He's just a friend, Vi," I said hoping to curtail that particular topic. Madge gave me a quizzical look, but Mignon looked relieved.

"Nice bow," Mignon stared in the direction of Hannibal who, upon seeing his next-door-nemesis retreated to his favorite corner.

"Want some taco salad?" Madge looked resentful of the intrusion.

"Sounds delightful," Mignon took two plates from the buffet. She served Vi first and then herself. "I think Madge puts too much sugar in her salad dressing, but otherwise this isn't a bad taco salad." She gave herself a mountain of the salad.

"Thanks." Madge snarled.

"So you're here for the Brunson meeting." I hoped Vi would join me in changing the subject.

"Indeed I am though I think it is absolutely pointless. It is a done deal. Taylor will become president and retain the majority of the shares."

"But you will have a hefty amount," Mignon smiled at her cousin. "We will all have enough to keep our dogs in kibble."

"I suppose. What do you suppose the ruckus was a few months ago that had all that whispering about a takeover and that sense of impending doom?

Remember Horace was in a positive twit?" Vi rubbed her massive diamond against her pants.

"What do you mean?" I asked.

"Nothing," Mignon shut off the conversation. "Horace was a type A who couldn't be rich enough. And if there had been something, it certainly doesn't matter now." She walked over to stare at Hannibal. "You would think an animal would grow on you."

"But if Horace was worried about something, then maybe it would help find his murderer." Forget talking about dogs, I'd never heard anything about dissention at Brunson Manufacturing, and it might just mean something to the murder investigation.

"It's nothing." Mignon said in a tone that, for the first time I could remember, had not very subtly told me to mind my own business.

Chapter Fourteen

I left for Kidstons' and the hated paint job very early. Since Jory was out of the picture, and since my house was no longer a safe house, I was out of it as much as I could be. The night before Suzi had left a message saying she was home and that Aaron had greeted her with two dozen yellow roses and tickets for a spring trip to Paris. All was well in the land of the rich and famous—for a while.

John Kidston greeted me at the door. "Caroline needed to get to a yoga make up lesson early. She said you know where everything is."

"I'll be fine." I smiled as I walked past him toward the dining room.

"It looks nice." He followed too closely behind as I prepared for a long day of painting.

"I think so too," I said. "I have a few touchups in this room, and then I can start on the baby's room." I kept my eyes on the rollers and paints as I talked.

"We're calling it a guest room." John said. "Caroline lost the baby last night."

"Oh, I am so sorry." John looked absolutely heartbroken. "Do you think she should be up and around already?"

"Dr. Newell told her to stay down for a while, but there's no stopping Caroline. She was going to see Maurice and then go to the club."

"I'll wait to hear what color she's thinking about for—the guest room." I stumbled over the room's new name.

"Good. She'll be back before you finish, I'm sure. Oh, and she said you want to give us the paint job as a gift. I won't accept that. You've already done a lot. Well, I'd better get to work." He picked up his computer bag and left. Once I was alone, sadness filtered through the beautiful house. I couldn't help wondering how much longer John and Caroline were going to be together. I also couldn't help wondering if that would at all change my feelings. Probably not. It was Jory I was missing. But it was Jory I had to forget about. I hadn't returned his calls, and when he stayed in Javier's car rather than come in, I knew he recognized things had changed between us.

The Kidstons' dining room has enormous floor to ceiling bay windows. As I administered a few last-minute touches, I had a sense that the snow outside was all around me. Christmas would be here before I knew it. All I wanted was to have the murders solved and to have my nice small town back the way it was.

I slathered the thick paint on and had to concede that it was turning out better than I thought, less a white than a mellow cream. I told myself that no one could have pulled it off but me. Maybe I'd put someone like Caroline in Harriet's story. However, it would be just like Caroline to recognize herself and sue me—using John for her lawyer, of course. No I'd go with my first inclination to create a nosy busybody named Flora. Too many hours of rolling paint gave me too many hours to think.

Why did Jory have to waltz into my boring life with the promise of something more! And why hadn't I told Whitey about what I saw that night? What excuse could Jory possibly give for trying to break into my house? And if I really thought Jory was the murderer wouldn't I have turned him in? Maybe something in me was telling me to trust him. Maybe.

As if to bring about some sort of cosmic joke, at that very second, Caroline Kidston returned with Whitey Barnes.

"Look who I found at my door," she said. "If you two will excuse me, I need to get changed."

"Hi, Whitey. I'd stop to talk but I'm very busy." I heard his heavy breathing as I concentrated on painting.

"E, I hear you're single again," he said. "I was wondering if you'd like to go to the Brunson Christmas party with me in a couple of weeks."

"Oh, Whitey, that's so nice of you," I turned to face him because I had no other choice, "but I'm going to be in Chicago that weekend visiting my college roommate." It wasn't a total lie, I might be.

"Too bad," he said as if he was more angry than disappointed. "I'm not giving up. And I'm glad you and Esqueda aren't dating. I don't trust that guy."

"We were just friends," I said feeling my face get red at the liberties he was taking. "I've got to ask, though, how you know we're not dating."

"Well, when I saw him Saturday Night at The Fireside with that hot little Hispanic number—I forget her name—I assumed you two were through."

"Oh, yes, Selma. They've been friends forever." I smiled so hard my face ached. "She's nice." I was weak kneed and sick at my stomach. It had nothing to do with paint fumes.

"I'm going to ask you out again." He made it sound more like a punishment than a promise. "Once these murders are solved, I'm going to be knocking on your door and calling until you say yes."

"Are you and the state police any closer to solving the crimes?" Again I had left Whitey three ideas behind.

"I can't talk about it, but there is a major break. Someone in Ann Arbor used to work for Brunson—an engineer—and he was caught selling dope there. My uncle was the guy who had to arrest him, and Horace was the guy who fired him."

"But how does that explain the break-ins at my house—and the Clara connection?"

"You said break-ins? Did you have another break-in?"

"I meant break-in," I said still unable to implicate Jory. "What about Clara's murder. How does the man in Ann Arbor connect to that?"

"He was fired, arrested, and sent to prison over a decade ago. He just got out a few months ago. I guess Clara's dad was the one who noticed that the guy had embezzled over two hundred thousand dollars through an accounting scheme with a friend of his. Mr. Nagel saw to it that the man left without his pension and his savings. He lost everything once he was caught stealing and selling."

"I can see why Horace felt protective of Clara if her father helped him keep the company coffers intact."

"I don't know anything about that."

"Well, I'd better get back to work." I climbed the ladder, aware that Whitey probably took in a long, yearning view of my rear before he left.

To my great delight, Caroline went out again and did not return all day. I was able to finish the room without her infectious depression. Though she would probably find half a dozen things wrong with the job I had done, I knew it was A-plus. Before I left, I called Earlene to see if she wanted to come for dinner. Bryce is the high school basketball coach—coach of the year for Michigan last year—and I knew she was probably going to eat alone. I was relieved that she said yes. I had some things I wanted to discuss with her.

Because I had sent Suzi home with the last of the Thanksgiving dinner, besides two pieces of left-over

Chicago style pizza and half a dozen of the world's best brownies, I wasn't sure I had enough food for two left so I stopped at The Fireside to get some of their legendary sausage lasagna, house salad and garlic sticks to go. I also stopped at the store for a good bottle of Chianti.

It was a little after seven when Earlene arrived with her effervescent smile and a shocking announcement. "Something happened a little while ago at the Kidstons'," she said pulling off her jacket. "Whitey stopped at John's office and drove him home."

"I was just there today—painting at their house," I said, thinking that I hoped Caroline hadn't tripped over a roller I had accidentally left. No one would believe it was an accident. "Do you mind if I call there?"

Earlene started setting the table as I tried several times to get something beyond the answering machine at the Kidstons'. It was probably nothing. Remember, it's Whitey who has a way of making even the tiniest, most insignificant fact seem like it belongs in *The Guinness Book of World Records.*

"Thanks." Earlene drank her wine as we both finished way too much of the rich, melted cheese and wine-flavored lasagna. "I am tired of eating alone."

"You and Bryce are all right, right?" I wasn't about to have another friend exhibit cracks in her marital union.

"We are perfect. I married the greatest guy in the world. We both work too much, though. However, I may have a very big announcement in a few days," she beamed so widely that there was no secret what the announcement was going to be. "Even if you think you know, don't ask me about it for a couple of days," she begged. "Then as soon as I've told Bryce and my mother, I'll tell you."

"I'll keep my fingers crossed." My mind shot to Caroline Kidston's miscarriage and then to why John had rushed out of the office. I hoped she wasn't having trouble as a result of the miscarriage. The doctor had told her not to tire herself, and she'd spent the day running all over town.

"And now let's talk about your love life? Are you and that hot to trot lawn guy still an item?"

"Jory? No, we were just friends. We had fun for a while, but it kind of just ran its course."

"The look on your face right this minute tells me that you and he were much more than that. E, I thought you might have found Mr. Right right here." She took a brownie and watched for my reaction.

"Wrong. No Mr. Right. Jory is indeed steamy, but he has way too many secrets."

"How do you mean?" Earlene studied me with a very serious look on her face.

"I mean he was always coming and going with no explanation. I think his secrets are dark and dangerous." I was so glad to get it off my chest, to tell someone my worst fears regarding the man I was having a hard time forgetting.

"E," Earlene reached across the table and took my wrist. "Do you trust me?"

"You know I do. What's this about?"

"Trust me when I say you may have given up too quickly on Jory Esqueda."

"What do you know about this?"

"Nothing. I really know nothing, but I have a feeling that Jory still might be someone you shouldn't turn away from."

"I know you mean well, but I think that Jory is bad news."

"Just don't do anything final, ok?"

Shortly after that I changed the discussion and a while later, Earlene got a call from Bryce that he was home. She left. I put the dishes in the dishwasher, fed Howler too many leftovers, and ran a hard copy of the nearly ninety pages I had of Harriet's story. I was reading through them, thinking they were pretty darn good, when my doorbell rang. Because it was nearly ten o'clock, my hands went numb at the thought of a stranger on my porch. I turned on the porch light, looked out my window, and saw that the visitor was no stranger. Oddly, the sight of Jory unnerved me more than ever for a myriad of reasons.

"Hi," I said thinking that it was all I could do not to fall against that wonderful smell and thick chest. "Do you want to come in?"

"E, I need you to come with me." He wasn't the warm, supportive Jory I'd been missing.

"It's after ten. Howler and I are getting ready to go to bed."

"I want you to come with me to the Kidstons'."

"Why?" Fear walloped me.

"John Kidston's wife died today."

"What?" I knew instantly that Jory was telling the truth, but I also knew that I couldn't take back every hateful thought I'd ever had toward her.

"She killed herself—carbon monoxide poisoning. A neighbor across the street called it in."

"But I was there until nearly five. I would have known."

"Javier called me to get you because John Kidston said you were someone he could talk to. Javier's there now. I guess Mrs. Kidston was depressed over a miscarriage."

"That can't be. Jory, you don't know her, but she wouldn't have cared that much. And she was a tough lady."

"According to Javier, it's cut and dried. Will you come?"

"Let me put Howler out for a minute and then we'll go, ok?" Everything around me had become hazy and other-worldly.

"I guess Kidston's really a mess. He was supposed to be home earlier but is working on a merger for Brunson Spice that took longer than he wanted. He blames himself."

"Is there going to be an autopsy?"

"I don't think so," Jory helped me with my jacket sending tingles up and down my arms.

"Try to encourage one, ok? This doesn't sound right. I know there are times you can't tell when someone is depressed, but Caroline Kidston was not the type who would kill herself. In fact, I might see her as someone who could commit murder, but not to herself."

"It's up to the husband, I think. You talk to him and see what he says."

"Ok."

The short drive to Clovelly Road seemed to take forever since Jory and I said nothing to each other. After all, what was there to say? What were you doing climbing down from my attic? How's Selma? I felt myself getting angry all over again until I thought about John and what he must be going through.

Police cars and a hearse were parked in front of Caroline's perfectly presented portico. I was sick all over thinking that she was actually dead. In our town of murders everywhere, I had forgotten that people died in other ways. But suicide? Caroline Kidston's parking herself in her luxury sedan and gassing herself was as improbable as my developing a penchant for rock climbing. Something was very wrong with this picture.

When we arrived, Jory joined Javier in the kitchen where the man I recognized as the county coroner and several other state police officers were going over forms. John was in the living room slumped in a chair, head bent.

"Johnny," I used the name I hadn't used since we were in elementary school.

"E, it's all my fault." He didn't raise his head. "She was miserable and instead of helping her, I got angrier and angrier. How am I ever going to call her father? Oh, god, she was all he had."

"Mr. Kidston," Javier stood next to us. "I'm sorry to interrupt, but did your wife have a drinking problem. We've found four times the legal limit in her bloodstream."

John rose, his hands shaking, his face ashen. "In the past few months, I noticed that she was drinking much more heavily. I knew it wasn't' good for the baby, but she wouldn't listen."

"That's ok," Javier patted his shoulder. "We just need to make sure that this isn't out of the ordinary. Sometimes, when people drink too much, they do something they wouldn't ordinarily do."

"See, John? It wasn't your fault. You are such a good guy. You've always been a good guy." I leaned my head against his. I hated him to see him in such agony.

"E," Jory was suddenly in front of us. "I'm going to have to leave. Javier will take you home when you're ready to go."

"Thanks. I'll walk you out."

"That's ok. You need to be here." Jory left with totally the wrong impression.

"What I hate most," John said tears flooding his face, "is that she was so scared, and I did so little to stop it. And then she lost the baby." He fell back into the chair, hiding his face in his hands.

"We're all afraid right now, John. And I'm sure you did all you could do. And there could have been other babies." I sat on the arm of the chair and put my arm around his neck.

"No. She seemed so unconcerned yesterday after the miscarriage that I told her maybe we should rethink the marriage before we made plans for another child. You know she and I were never the perfect couple." He looked up at me with eyes that could melt Lot's wife.

"John, you need to listen to me. I have known you longer and better than almost anyone. You did everything you could to make your marriage work, and I'm sure that what you and Caroline said to each other in the heat of anger was just that—the heat of anger. You were more than your fights and threats, ok? We all say things we wish we hadn't. We all do things we wish we could take back." My mind's eye saw Jory walking out the door a few minutes earlier. "Now, you need to call Caroline's father, and I'll stay here while you do that. Then you'll have to call your parents. They're still in Florida, aren't they?"

"Europe. They left Boca for a month's trip to Europe. What a rotten thing I'm about to do to them."

"First things first," I said as I went about guiding John to make the call to Caroline's father. It was a fairly short call, and when John returned from making it, he stared at me.

"Do you know what he said?" John was in shock, his face drained of all color and his motions robotic. "He said, 'Oh, god, just like her mother.' Caroline's mother committed suicide. E, she never told me that. Can you imagine being married to someone and skipping that little fact?" John's grief was being replaced by anger. "I didn't know her. I would get to the point that I thought I did, and then there would be one of those little secrets—like her drinking. He wants the memorial service to be there. Can you help me with the funeral home and obituary?"

How could I not? Whether I liked it or not, I was smack in the middle of John Kidston's life once more. He'd helped me through the toughest funeral of my life. Now I'd help him.

It was hours before John finished talking to the police and directing the coroner as to his plans. "Her father wants her buried in Boston and then put in the family plot there. I'm going to go along with it. It's the least I can do for him—and her. We'll do a little visitation here at the house for her Camphor friends."

Javier drove me home. "You and Jory aren't seeing each other right now?" He asked as I fastened my belt. "Lucy is upset, thinks you two were good together."

"I did too," I said too emotionally raw from the terrible evening to mask my feelings, "but Jory is a man of many secrets, secrets he doesn't share. And then there's Selma."

"Selma? She's not in this. Oh, Mama Esqueda is plenty mad, but Selma is going to marry one of my buddies. You know that other guy that was there tonight? The other state trooper? He popped the question and Selma is happy as can be. Jory took her out the other night to congratulate both of them. Lucy, Dave, and I met them after work. Look it's not my business, no way, no how, but he's been nuts about you since you were in high school. You are the girl of his dreams, kid." He patted my shoulder as I opened the door to go in the house.

"Thanks," I said, "but some mountains are too high to climb."

"E, don't close any doors," Javier said as he opened mine and led me into the dark house. "Things have been wild in this town. Let everything settle down."

"Whitey says that may be soon, that you have a suspect."

"Had a suspect," Javier said as he finished checking the house. "His alibi checks out and about a thousand Mormons—his new church—support his claim that he is a changed man. I don't think he's our killer."

"And you're sure that Caroline Kidston killed herself and isn't another victim?"

"It's textbook suicide, E," he said.

Chapter Fifteen

I slept sporadically, waking several times, sure that I heard strange sounds. Suddenly I was all grown up. The pleasant memories of childhood were ripped away by the tortured look on John Kidston's face. My heart beat wildly, and I would have been sure I was in the middle of a heart attack if I didn't see it for what it was: panic brought on by irreparable entrapment. I didn't want to be the woman who would help John through his torment. I didn't want to say goodbye to Jory. I didn't want to be the unsuccessful mediator between Madge and Mignon, and I most certainly didn't want to live anywhere that murder was just around the corner.

At five thirty, I roused, made a cup of coffee, brushed my teeth and pulled on my work clothes. Only then did I realize that there was no work. My latest job had been obliterated with the death of Caroline Kidston. I let a sleepy-eyed Howler out and poured myself another cup of coffee. As I was sitting back in the same kitchen chair I had sat in every time my mother and I had one of our humorous and heartwarming conversations, I saw a movement on the back porch. "Howler, come here," I whispered as he started to nose around the doorway. Get over here." I looked in the direction of the phone, across the long kitchen and in view of the many windows my mother had put in so she could feel encircled by woods and trees.

"E." A knock and whisper let me know it was Jory, but I still wasn't sure I should open the door. What if my worst fears were right about him? With Whitey tied up in the Kidston suicide, the police would be otherwise engaged.

"Jory, I'm pretty tired," I opened the door a bit to very reluctantly close the door on our relationship. He pushed past, putting my heart on red alert. Maybe I was having a heart attack.

"This is against my better judgment," he said as he poured himself a cup of coffee without permission. "But when I saw you with Kidston, I knew I had to do something."

"We're just friends." And at that moment looking into Jory's irresistible, loving face, I knew I was telling him and myself the absolute truth. John and I were dear, longtime friends, but no matter how hard I tried I'd never been able to summon the feelings for John that surfaced every time I saw or thought about Jory.

"It doesn't matter. I know how he feels about you— and I know how I feel about you. Here take this coffee, and I'll warm yours up. Sit."

Just as Howler does when he wants a biscuit, I sat on command. "I need to tell you something before you go into a long explanation," I said. "I saw you breaking into my house the other night. I don't see how you can explain your way out of that."

"Let's go back to the beginning, ok? You can check everything I'm telling you with Javier. He's the one who urged me to come clean."

"Javier knows about this?" I said.

"He's the one who got me into it." Jory drank from the cup that had moments before been mine. "It started my last year in the Air Force. I came home for Christmas. Dad had died the summer before, and I was talking about what I was going to do. Of course Mama urged me to take over the landscaping business. Javier had been working two jobs, so had Lucy, and we all knew they couldn't keep that up. None of us wanted to see all my father's work go down the drain. But law school, not gardening, was my dream."

"No offense, Jory, but there's a long way from the lawn care business to skulking around in my yard."

"Exactly," he said, serious and more appealing than ever. I wanted to dive across the table and begin kissing him. I didn't. "Javier told me about a part-time undercover group in The State Police. He said with my special ops training, I was made for it. The group was formed right after September 11 and works with Homeland Security. The idea is to give small towns like Camphor extra investigative and surveillance help when something bad happens. It helps pay my way through law school and lets me do the lawn business. I can't tell anyone because that would destroy the group's purpose."

"It sounds absolutely preposterous," I said. "It has to be true. And I am so glad." I took his hands in mine. "But how did you end up in my yard?"

"Watching for terrorists frequently gives me a birds' eye view of other things—like Whitey getting that buckshot in his rear and Glen Newell sneaking into Mignon's about three times a week."

"Three times! I'm amazed. I knew they did their little thing once in a while, but three times a week! They're too old for that!"

"My chica, you are never too old." He rose and came to me with heat and what must be love. "I couldn't stand watching you touch him tonight." He met my kisses with his own, more demanding, more searing.

"Wait. Before this leads where I know it will," I stopped him as he started to pull my sweatshirt over my head. "You still haven't told me how you ended up in my yard."

"It was an accident. I was out and about doing my state police thing when I happened to wander over here. I think I wanted to make sure you weren't two-timing me." He took a long pause to pull me close and kiss me. "I saw you in the den working on your computer. But the moon was enormous so I saw a figure in your attic. I couldn't let you know what I was doing scouring the neighborhood so I scaled the tree next to your window and started to climb in. Whoever was in the attic must have heard me because he started down the tree kicking me and knocking me to the ground. I was stunned for a minute but got up and started chasing him. So you see, I wasn't technically trespassing. I never made it to your attic."

"What a relief." I put my arms around him and kissed him forever.

Ice cold soda over crushed ice on a hot day. That's the best way I can describe what I felt with Jory that night. Relief flowed over me, longing was replaced by a sense of being fully and forever loved. "Tell me," he whispered, "that I'm never going to have to worry about John Kidston and you. I really hated it, and I hated myself for feeling so jealous of a guy who is at the lowest point of his life."

"John's just a dear old friend. You are not a friend." Then I proved my point over and over.

"But don't you have a confession or two? Selma?" I asked when we were done making our points.

"Oh, Selma. That's such a sad story. If you can believe this, she has forsaken me for a friend of Javier's. Can you imagine anyone doing that?"

"I certainly can't." I started to kiss him again when the phone rang.

"Hello, John. How are you? What can I do?" I watched Jory for a reaction to John's early morning call but all I saw was desire. "Sure. Let me get my shower, and I'll be over there," I told him.

"He ok?"

"He sounds groggy—like he's either taken something to sleep or hasn't slept. I told him I'd be over soon."

"After our shower, right?" He pulled me up and into the shower which was a whole lot more fun with Jory than alone.

"I have work to do and then I'd like to take you to a romantic dinner later, after you've done what you need to help your 'old friend'." We were dressed and in the kitchen.

"Dinner would be lovely. Could we stop in at the ladies' though before we eat? I know Caroline's suicide will throw them into a tizzy. And you can meet Tiffany and Hannibal."

"Who?"

"I'll explain later. Now scoot." I left for John's without a cup of coffee or a sense of where the day would take me.

The Kidston house was full of people when I got there. Caroline's father had arrived on the redeye. He looked smaller, less important, but when I shook his hand and expressed my condolences, he stood straight, remained composed, and thanked me. To the end, he would remain in control.

"I am too old to go through this again," he said and then turned to introduce me to the woman going over papers with John. "This is Celia Frey, my right arm."

By the way Celia looked at Caroline's father, I could see that he wouldn't have to go through his daughter's death alone. Celia looked up from what she'd been studying and stood to greet me. She was in her fifties and exhibited the kind of poise that very classy women always seem to possess.

"Celia has been helping me with Caroline's final arrangements. She will be immediately cremated." John said, obviously still in a state of shock. It was so hard to see him like that. "I didn't even know she wanted that."

"Who would have known," Celia said, "that she wouldn't have had more time to tell you?" She gently placed her hand on his arm.

"Right. E, we need some food for the service and some calls need to be made to old friends of Caroline's. Celia knows most of them and will give you a list of those she doesn't. Would you go to the deli for food?" John was going through the motions.

"You know I think I would use the country club if I were you. They have the best chef, and since you belong there, I'm sure they'll do whatever you need to accommodate you. Maybe little sandwiches and tarts?"

"That's good. Caroline would like that." He got up and stumbled to the kitchen returning with a pot of coffee and followed by one of his cousins holding half a dozen coffee cups.

All morning people came, and for a brief time in Camphor, suicide trumped murder. It was clear that friends of John and Caroline couldn't deal with how she had died. They referred to her "passing" or her "too short life." When it was all over, John and I would sit down and talk about how he felt about how Caroline had died. And hate me, but I also drifted back to the wonder of waking up next to Jory. I would remember to thank Javier for nudging the man I loved to come forward with the truth.

Maurice entered as I was about to fill the coffee cups. "Oh, E, this basket of cheeses is all I could come up with. She was a bit of a snot," Maurice kept his voice low, "but she and I served on the hospital board, and there were times she was helpful—very bright woman. Oh, and I see Celia is already here."

"You know Celia?" I was surprised.

"Sure. She handled all Caroline's legal matters so she was frequently there when money was given to the hospital or the Brunson Foundation. Caroline became quite a heavy contributor to the foundation."

I left Maurice to schmooze, and headed to the phone. I made calls to the list of people Celia had given me. Sadly, there wasn't an outpouring of grief or sympathy. Of course, I didn't tell them how she died. That was up to John. Then I called the chef at the country club. As I thought, he seemed the saddest of all. Caroline, he said, had been a frequent and generous patron. We arranged for thinly sliced sandwiches of salmon, beef and chicken on his homemade bread. There would also be the house specialty salad, crudités and a variety of cheesecakes. "Simple and classy," he said. "Mrs. Kidston would approve."

John's folks arrived mid afternoon so I was free to leave. "Come back tomorrow, ok?" he said, his eyes full of a need for me that I didn't want him to have.

"I will."

I knew I should have gone to the ladies' to tell them what had happened, but I went home and began writing. Harriet was in the middle of the third murder in town and no one was believing that the deaths were connected. A truck driver she knew from her days as a secretary was showing interest in her. This made her both happy and uncomfortable. He wanted more than friendship but was too curious as far as she was concerned. Besides, her heart already belonged to Scrap Sloan.

Suzi was also on my mind. I called her mid-morning but got no answer. She would want to know about Caroline Kidston. When I tried reaching her for the third time and failed, I called her at work. I was told she was no longer there.

No longer there. Suzi? She loved that job. Now I was afraid. I hadn't talked to her since she'd visited. And I had no idea where Aaron worked. I sat thinking about any names she'd given me that might help but in an instant I realized that I knew very little of Suzi's Chicago life. I hated to bother or worry her family, but I was desperate to know where she was.

"E, it's so good to hear from you," Suzi's mother's sister, frail-looking when I knew her in college, sounded even more frail. "What can I do for you?"

"I've been trying to reach Suzi," I said. "I keep getting her machine, and I want to tell her that the wife of an old friend died."

"Oh I'm so sorry. Let me know who it is, and I'll get in touch with her. She's gone away for a week or so. She said she needed a rest. She asked that only I have the number. I will, however, let her know you called."

"Then she's all right?" I was tons relieved.

"She is fine, dear. I'm sure she'll be in touch with you soon. I'm sorry to hear about your friend's wife."

I thanked her and said good-bye, glad I had made the call.

When I finished writing late in the afternoon, I had nearly ten chapters of a book I hated to stop working on. There was no explaining why Harriet Hudacre had become part of my life, but I felt I knew her as well as I knew the ladies. There was also no explaining the healing power of writing for me. At a time when I might be absolutely engulfed in panic, my story had given me a focus other than myself. No matter how bad things were in Camphor, they seemed much worse in Harriet's Crabtree, Virginia.

Speaking of which, as I poured a soda, I looked out the kitchen window to see one of the wildest sights I'd seen in Camphor. There they were, Madge and Midge, walking their pooches. Mignon--always the picture of decorum--walked slowly with little Tiffany, trotting along in a perfect heel. When Mignon stopped, eager-to-please Tiffany stopped too. They had on matching black fur jackets. Half a block in front of them were Madge and Hannibal. Though it was obvious, Madge, too, was working on heel, it was on her heels that Hannibal was tripping. She would tug on the leash and shout something loudly enough that I could almost hear it in the house, but Hannibal, wearing a red bandana with his Brillo pad hair standing inches away from his head, first sat looking stunned and then when Madge tugged him toward her, he wound himself around her trying to win her affection. It was a circus with Mignon and Tiffany stopping frequently. When Mignon shook her head, I swear Tiffany seemed to do the same. Maybe I was just tired. Anyway, there was no need to visit the ladies until Jory and I went out that evening.

"Let me know what I can do for John," Earlene said when she stopped at little before six that night. I had just finished getting ready for dinner. "My you look very hot," she said.

"I have a date."

"Oh you do. And may I ask if this date is the same man you and I have discussed."

"Maybe." I felt a blush creeping across my face that would confirm all Earlene's suspicions.

"Very good decision. If there's one thing Caroline's death has taught us it is that life can be unexpectedly short. Let's not waste time."

"I agree."

"And I have been searching for those files you asked about. I may have something tomorrow. I'll stop by after work instead of your coming to my office, if that's all right."

"Be careful," I said.

"My mama didn't raise no dummies," she laughed and left.

Maybe because Mignon loves me, maybe because she knows when to fold 'em, or maybe Tiffany has made her a changed person, whatever the reason I was grateful that she greeted Jory warmly when we stopped in before dinner.

"She's cute," he said bending down to pet Tiffany's silky ears.

"Isn't she?" Mignon smiled at Jory as if he were her long-lost son. Who knew all it would take was a three pound ball of fuzz, or several bottles of wine for my old friend to warm up to the love of my life.

"I thought we should stop over to see if you've heard about Caroline Kidston." I picked up Tiffany who worked her sharp little teeth on my thumb.

"Maurice called me several hours ago. You know I am very conflicted because I doubt that I've said one nice thing or had one kind thought, which Madge reminded me when I called to tell her of Caroline's death."

"You are certainly not the first to say something bad about Caroline Kidston. She was a tough one to love. But we love John, and he knows we wouldn't have wanted this to happen. Maurice was kind enough to stop by John's with a basket."

"He seemed to have a little bit of a friendship with her—they worked together over some Brunson things."

"Well, John is a mess and will need all of his friends," I said watching Jory stroke Tiffany and wishing those long fingers were roaming over my body.

"Can I get you two something?" she asked. "This is Sally's day off so she left me with a variety of tasty things and some interesting teas."

"No thanks. We're on our way to dinner." I rose to leave when Madge burst through the door, followed by her raggedy, splay-legged friend.

"Oh no, that dog can't come in here," Mignon picked up Tiffany.

"Oh don't be so high and mighty. I came over to see if E knows anymore about Caroline Kidston—oh, hi, Jory. " Madge's hair had taken on a finger-stuck-in-a-light-socket cache.

"Hello, Mrs. Bobik. So this is Hannibal." Jory petted his chest motioning for the dog to jump. On his hind legs, Hannibal nearly matched Jory's six feet.

"Don't encourage him." Mignon held Tiffany to her bosom as if it might be their last minutes on earth.

"I have an idea." Jory moved quickly from where he was sitting to the table on which Hannibal's leash was lying. "E, how 'bout if you visit for a few minutes and I'll take this guy for a walk. Do you want that, fella?" Hannibal's licking tongue and wiggling tail said he loved Jory almost as much as I did.

"Thanks so much. I can tell he trusts you." Madge gushed. Jory had added another adoring member to his entourage.

"You can take Tiffany for a walk sometime too," Mignon said not to be outdone.

"Glad to," Jory shouted over his shoulder as the dog pulled him out the door.

"What a nice man," Madge said. "They said you can't fool kids and animals, and Hannibal loves him."

"Hannibal sees him as a nice juicy piece of meat," Mignon said still clinging to Tiffany. "The dog is a walking nightmare."

"You know," I said, "I think we've been through enough awful things in the past few weeks to start being a little kinder to each other, don't you? You both have great dogs. Treat each other better or I'm through."

They stared at me as if I were the hatchet murderer.

"You don't mean it," Madge coaxed in her childlike way. "You wouldn't give up on us."

"You know you love us like you love those lattes of yours."

"Maybe," I said, "but I won't encourage your bad behavior."

"Oh, E," Madge wept, "you sound just like your mother. Doesn't she sound like Catherine, Mignon?"

"She does." Even the crusty Mignon's eyes had filled with tears.

"Vi left before we got word of Caroline. I'm glad, too. She is coming to think of Camphor as the Wild Midwest. And, of course, there were no surprises at the board meeting—except perhaps one." Mignon poured Madge and me cups of tea.

"Look, isn't she just adorable." Mignon looked at the corner of the sofa into which Tiffany had tucked herself. "How did I live without her?"

"Well, don't step on her with those size elevens of yours—oops, sorry," Madge's face showed only a hint of sincerity. "She is little though."

"No one will step on her. You said there was a surprise at the board meeting?" I said.

"Not a surprise to me," Mignon said, "because I've been watching his finagling. Maurice was voted onto the board. Though it was a bit against my better judgment, I voted for him, and everyone else did too. I guess everyone realizes that the senior generation of Brunsons is dwindling—and lord knows that Taylor will need help. He's lived in that rarefied air of the university community for way too long. I'm not sure he's touched reality in years. And Glen Newell is the only non-Brunson we can trust not to want to go public. The four other non-Brunson board members seem to have less and less loyalty to the company."

"Did Maurice really want that?" I was surprised. "I mean, it seems as if he's done everything he can to avoid being part of Brunson Spice."

"Oh I don't think it was Brunson Spice he minded. It's more the Brunson family. He and Horace were particularly contentious."

"That's interesting." I saw Jory and Hannibal coming up the walk so all thoughts of Maurice were shoved out of the way.

"This is a great animal," Jory said as he removed Hannibal's leash. "I'll take him for a walk anytime."

"Oh he is so smart." Madge beamed and then bent down to let Hannibal lick her entire face.

"Oh don't let him do that," Mignon said. "He is full of germs."

"Your mouth is dirtier than this dog's," Madge said defiantly.

"I'll leave you to round three," I said as Jory helped put on my jacket. "We're going off to dinner."

"Would you mind," I asked as we pulled into the parking lot of The Fireside, "getting some Chinese and sitting by the fire instead?"

"Have I told you that you are totally a girl after my own heart?" Jory said. "I'm not up for an audience tonight." He kissed my cheek and put his truck in reverse. Just then I noticed Maurice and one of his young associates disembark from his limousine. "How well do you know him?" Jory said, his eyes glued to Maurice.

"Very well and not at all," I laughed. "It seems as if he's been around forever—at the parties my parents gave and the ones he gave. When my father died, he was especially attentive to my mother and me. In fact, I thought he might be in love with my mother—I was young and didn't realize how impossible that would be. Why do you ask?"

"Not sure. Just wondered."

Maurice? We were getting desperate for suspects when artsy-fartsy Maurice Brunson was considered below suspicion.

"Is there something I should know?" I leaned against his shoulder as he drove to Li's Chinese To Go.

"All you need to know is that no one can be totally trusted until we get the murderer. We have some new evidence and that has given us answers and opened up a lot of questions."

"Did you learn something about Clara Nagel?"

"I can't say much, but Javier is working on it. When he says it's ok, I'll tell you. Now, do you mind if I stop at my mother's for a change of clothes before we go to your place?"

"Hey, aren't you taking a lot for granted?"

"Chica, with you, I take nothing for granted. There's no way you're sleeping alone, though. You need protection."

"Yes," I smiled, "let's not forget protection."

Jory's mother's house was across town, a large duplex with a fence that ran the length of the spacious lot. "I'm out of here next month. My house will be ready. I'll take you over there to get ideas for furniture, ok?"

"Fine, but you can tell from how little I've done to my own place, I'm not the world's best decorator."

"I want you to be comfortable there," he said in a way that totally thrilled me.

"There's your mother." I said with trepidation as I saw a woman pacing back and forth in her living room.

"Just put up with her for a minute. I'll be back in record time. Unless you want to sit in the car?"

"I can't. She sees me and would take my not coming in for rudeness."

"You're probably right. Hey, Mama," he bent to kiss his mother. "You remember E?"

"Hello, Miss Clary." Mrs. Esqueda tried to work up a smile but her hostility toward me contorted into a house-of-mirrors twist downward. Yep, she still hated me.

"You have such a lovely house," I said as I looked around at the delicate Mexican figurines.

"Thank you. Are you and Jory going out?"

"We're going to get dinner." Where was he? This was excruciating.

"You are welcome to stay here for dinner. Lucy and Javier are coming by."

"Thanks, Mama, but we've already made dinner plans." Jory rushed into the room. His mother gave his dop kit and duffle bag serious scrutiny.

"Then you won't be back tonight?" she asked.

"I don't think so. Well, we'd better go."

"Goodbye." I said. She said nothing because I was sure she was struggling to keep from shouting "whore!"

"Maybe bringing your extra clothes out in front of your mother was not such a good idea. I'm not exactly winning her heart and mind."

"Well, you've won mine and that's all that matters." He jumped into the truck and pulled me next to him. "Mama's not in love with you but I am."

And after Chinese and wine in front of the fire, Jory and I spent time doing what we'd both hungered to do for quite a while. We fit. His body was a perfect match for mine. Oriental rugs in front of a warm fire have many uses, practical and otherwise.

Chapter Sixteen

"I have to go to Grand Rapids this morning. Want to ride along?" Jory asked as I made the one breakfast dish I feel comfortable with: Spanish omelet. "Hey, this is good."

"I would love to ride with you but I'm supposed to meet Earlene at her office—in about fifteen minutes. Then I just may write."

"And when can I read this book of yours."

"Wait until I'm done, ok?"

"Ok. Well, I'm off." He took me into his arms and kissed me long and tenderly. "I suppose you're going over to Kidstons', too. Watch yourself."

"I will. And you have nothing to worry about. John is grief stricken, and I'm in love." I'd said it before I thought about it, and because of that knew I was right. I had waited a long time to have that feeling my mother had described to me so many years ago. Jory was it for me.

"I will take you to dinner tonight." He kissed me again and left.

Then, happier than I'd ever remembered being, with more to look forward to than I could imagine, panic attacked every pore. I was dizzy and couldn't catch my breath. Nothing was in focus and if it hadn't happened so many times before, I would have been worried. Panic can come when you're extremely depressed, afraid, or happy. This time it was definitely going after the latter. It came unbidden and totally unpredictably. I sat and hoped that within a few minutes and with enough breathing in an out, I would regain my stability, and, sure enough, slowly I began to feel like myself. I left for Earlene's feeling a little off kilter but knew that just might be how I would always feel.

John's office was locked with a notice that said he would be back in two weeks. Earlene's office was just down the hall from it.

"I'm not sure we should even be meeting here," she said. "I started looking for those missing files in a storage room here at the bank. I think I found some that may be they. They were at the bottom of a pile of trash. I don't think they've been touched for forty years."

"How do you know they're the files that someone might have been searching for?" I looked at the dusty, dog-eared manila folders.

"This." She pointed to a file that said Brunson Transfer 1968.

"Did you look through them?"

"Yes, and there is something totally unexplained. In 1968, one fifth of the Brunson Spice stocks were given to an anonymous recipient."

"Given?" I knew that even in those days that much Brunson stock would have been worth millions.

"And there are witnesses to the transfer. Your father was one. Horace Brunson was another. And Randall Kidston was the third. Did your family ever talk about this? E, this is a lot of stock."

"I have no idea what went on here. And I also have no idea how we can find out."

"What about Maurice Brunson?" Earlene put the files in her attaché. "Maybe he knows something. Until then, I'll keep these with me."

"I wish I knew if this had anything to do with Clara's murder and everything else."

"Just ask Maurice."

"I think Jory wants me to be careful where Maurice is concerned, as if he could be a threat!" Ridiculous.

"Maurice is featherweight. I see no way that he is dangerous." Earlene laughed.

"You're right. Jory is just overprotective. I'll try to see him today."

I didn't have to wait long to see Maurice because his limo was in front of John's house when I pulled up. My little Toyota looked forlornly out of place next to the limo and BMWs. "Don't worry. I love you." I said patting its rusty hood.

A well-dressed, poised older woman introduced to me as Caroline's aunt led me to the kitchen where a much more composed John was talking to Maurice and several others I didn't recognize.

"Oh, E, I'm glad you're here. We've been finalizing plans for Saturday. Maurice has graciously volunteered to go through Caroline's things and pull out anything that might be important. Her father and I can't force ourselves to do it."

"That's very nice," I said, wondering if it was. Then I remembered Earlene's certainty that Maurice was not a threat. "Would you like me to help?"

"If you would like, my dear." In a camel cashmere sports coat and slacks with a purple silk turtle neck, Maurice seemed a bit subdued. "I think this is all very sad." He said as we walked to the den which Caroline also used as an office.

"I hear you're a new Brunson board member," I said. "How did they coerce you? I thought that was the last thing you would want."

Maurice stopped at the door of the den. "I am a Brunson." He was surprisingly curt.

"Of course you are." I left the subject.

Caroline had three, three-drawer files. One was marked Foundation Business and Charities. Another was dedicated to her activities with the University of Michigan and her Chi Omega sorority. The last was marked Miscellaneous.

"How about if you take the Michigan one?" Maurice asked. "I'll take this one." He began rooting through the one marked Miscellaneous.

Since I had no idea what I was looking for, I wandered from file to file. It was clear that Caroline had been exceedingly generous with the university as well as active in supporting their fundraising. She had been equally generous and active where her sorority was concerned.

I couldn't help noticing that Maurice was moving through the drawers of his file much faster, as if he knew exactly what he was looking for.

"Are you looking for something special?" I asked as his fingers deftly flipped through the files.

"John thinks something was bothering Caroline these past months. Perhaps there is a clue here?"

"Did he say what it might be?"

"No, but he thought that ever since Clara Nagel was found dead, Caroline seemed distracted and disconnected." He returned to rifling through the files.

For the next hour or so, I sifted through the most boring correspondence and activities known to woman. Caroline's life made my painting world look thrilling by comparison. I guess you can be too rich and too thin. Caroline's world was reduced to clubs and foundation meetings.

"E, are you just about done here?" John asked. "I need you in the living room."

"Sure." I shut the last file drawer and left with John. Maurice was still diligently searching folders.

John and the minister were going over quotes and Bible passages. I helped them pick out some that would have satisfied the private woman whose death had sent another shock wave through Camphor. As we talked, delivery vans loaded with flowers pulled up.

John's mother and father also arrived and were busy greeting people and doing whatever their son needed. Seeing Randall Kidston reminded me of the folder that Earlene had slid into her attaché.

"E, my dear, it is so good of you to have helped John through this tragic time." John's father greeted me with the same warmth I had come to count on from him. "I'm only sorry it has taken us so long to get here. We had a much longer layover at JFK than we'd planned on."

"John seems to be holding up." I looked at the man who was one hundred percent better than he'd been the previous night. "I was wondering if you have a minute?"

"Certainly." Tall and stately with a shock of white hair that fell over his forehead, Randall Kidston was an older, heavier version of his son. "What is it you need?"

"I'm curious about something and thought perhaps you could help." As I told him about the stolen files, his face went from placid to rigid.

"E, that was all a very long time ago, and I'm certain that your father would not want me to divulge what those files contained. We were sworn to secrecy."

"Who was sworn to secrecy?" Maurice had joined us.

"No one." I said, hoping that Randall Kidston would take my cue.

"We were just talking about Caroline," Randall said. "It's still too much for Loretta and me to take in."

"Oh," Maurice said. "I'll be on my way. It looks like there was nothing there." As he left, I noticed that something was making a bulge in his pocket, something that hadn't been there when we began our search of

Caroline's files. Maybe Maurice, too, had more secrets than he was willing to share.

"Everything is set at the club. And I've made arrangements to have the flowers delivered to the church in Boston an hour or so before the service," I said as I hugged John good-bye.

"Will you be back?" he asked.

"Not tonight. I have a date." I didn't want him to attach too much to my helping him through a terrible time.

Howler was hungry when I got home so even though it was hours before his supper, I fed him. I fed me too. Then I ran cold water over some jumbo shrimp that had been in the freezer for lord knew how long, chopped up an avocado and red onion to mix with the shrimp. At the end I mixed a bit of lemon juice, olive oil, salt and pepper and threw it over my concoction. Tasty. It would hold me until dinner with Jory.

Earlene was at my back door ready to knock when I opened it for Howler.

"What are you doing back here?" I laughed.

"E, I just got a call from Bryce. His team was an alternate for the math Olympics in Lansing. One of the finalists has been disqualified, which means he'll be going—tonight. He needs me to go along as a chaperone."

"He must be elated. We need to celebrate as soon as you're back. My treat."

"Love to. Right now, though, my big worry is this." She pulled out the files. "I need you to hold onto them. Maybe you should even give them to the police."

"Not necessary. I'll take care of them—put them where no one could find them, though I'm not sure where that would be right now."

"Thanks. I don't feel comfortable leaving them in the house when I'll be gone. And I can't take them with me with all those kids around. Who knows what could happen. I did mention to Whitey that I had some papers he needed to look at but that I couldn't see him until Monday."

"No problem. Go and have a great time. We'll talk when you get back."

Earlene left Howler and me with hours to go before Jory would be back from Grand Rapids. I thought about heading toward the ladies' but they walked by, dogs in tow in a strange, discordant rhythm of pulling and pushing their dogs. Tiffany was still the perky little performer while Hannibal seemed confused as to why his owner had put a long piece of leather around his neck and saw fit to control him with it. He was still yards ahead of his mistress.

Because I didn't want a return of the panic I'd experienced earlier, I grabbed my laptop and returned to Harriet's story. Even I, a totally self-critical and insecure writer, thought my mystery just might have a chance. And Suzi knew an editor. Suzi. What was going on in her life anyway?

At four o'clock the doorbell rang. It was Mama Esqueda. "Jory thought you might like these," she stepped inside and unveiled a pan of delicious-looking enchiladas. "I make them at the beginning of the week and give them to people who might like them."

She still wasn't smiling but she wasn't spitting tacks either.

"They look absolutely delicious," I took the pan from her. "Come in and have some tea." I wasn't going to let this hopeful moment pass.

I took her coat and guided her to the kitchen. "And I have these great brownies." I put several on a plate. "They're from Chicago and are delicious."

"Nice." She took a bite of the brownie which seemed to live up to expectations. "Good tea."

"Thanks." I was ready to bask in the glory of the moment when a crackling sound from the living room alerted me to danger. "Stay here." I said as I moved quickly to see what was going on.

Another crackling sound stopped me dead in my tracks. Gunshots. Someone was shooting at me! I grabbed a terrified-looking Mrs. Esqueda and yelled for Howler to follow as I headed for the stairs, staying low and motioning for Mama Esqueda to do the same. "We're going to my room. My cell phone is there. Do you know Javier's number."

"I-I-think so." Jory's mother looked as panicked as I'd ever been. "What is happening?"

"We'll be ok. I promise." I got the three of us inside the room and locked the door. I heard the glass on the back door break and knew whoever was causing the trouble was on his way after us. "What's the number?"

I dialed as she gave me the number. "Javier, it's E. Get somebody over here. We're being shot at. Your mother-in-law is with me." Javier said to stay safe and that someone would be there immediately.

"You're dead. Get out here and maybe you'll be able to stay alive." It was a voice I didn't recognize.

"Go away," I screamed. "Leave us alone."

A gunshot in the area of the doorknob shattered some wood and compromised the lock. This could be the end of my life.

Sirens. Many sirens. Then the voice from outside said "Shit" and ran down the stairs. We were safe.

"Oh, Javi," Mrs. Esqueda ran to her son-in-law. "This is an awful place."

As I told Javier what had happened, I caught Mrs. Esqueda's look. I was definitely persona non grata again. She held the pan of enchiladas tightly against her chest. I may have survived the attack, but I had lost the war with Jory's mother.

"Do you have any idea what prompted this?" Javier asked.

"You know I think I do. It might have been these. Oh no..." I had left the folders on the table and they were gone. "They were after some folders that Earlene Banks found. She left them with me, but they're gone. Who would know to come here?"

Javier shook his head. "My men chased someone into the field at the end of town but lost him."

"E?" Jory burst into the kitchen totally ignoring his mother who clung to him and wept voluminously.

"I'm fine. You need to look after your mother," I pointed toward the frantic woman. "She got a lot more than she bargained for when she brought me some wonderful enchiladas." I smiled at her trying to re-ignite the spark of friendship that had been there earlier. It was crystal clear, though, that Mrs. Esqueda was now firmly convinced I was a leper who posed a threat to everyone she loved.

"Mama, you will be fine. E, come with me. You're going to stay with us."

Everything but Mrs. Esqueda's voice shouted "No! You can't stay with us." Her son was oblivious to his mother's signals. "Right, Mama?"

"Right." Mrs. Esqueda was far from a master liar.

"I'm going to stay with Madge, but thanks anyway," I said to Mrs. Esqueda's loud sigh of relief. "She has a great alarm system and a huge watchdog."

"I don't feel good about this."

"No worry. No one will do anything again today. But I don't feel like dinner." Every fiber in me was exhausted. I had suddenly run out of all the juice that made me go. Panic, stress, fear, anger—they all met in a dance in my head. Aspirin and bed. That was suddenly my prescription for happiness. "Take your mom home and call me later."

Jory didn't leave until I called Madge and let her know what was happening. Later I'd have to make excuses about why I'd called Madge instead of Mignon, but Hannibal was truly part of the reason.

There was someone who found Hannibal more distasteful than Mignon. That someone was Howler. When Hannibal rose his tired body to sniff and greet his guest, my dog growled and slunk off.

"Howler!" I said, probably feeling the way a young mother does when her child punches a little kid in front of her. "I'm so sorry Madge."

"Howler's been through a lot. You both have."

Madge called The Fireside and ordered two small filets, salads, butternut squash and Death-by-Chocolate, their unbelievably rich and sumptuous dessert— chocolate mousse, Heath bars, chocolate cake and whipping cream all in one. Oh, yes, and sprinkled with Kahlua, what's not to like? Even I, in my state of exhaustion and fear, ate the entire meal.

"Now you come upstairs with me..." Madge started to say when the doorbell rang.

"Are you two having a party?" Mignon asked. "I saw Jory leave E off. I would have come over then, but I saw that you ordered dinner and I wasn't invited."

"Get over yourself," Madge snapped. "E was shot at tonight."

"Shot at!" Mignon fell back into a chair. "Are you sure?"

"I have the bullet holes to prove it." I said. "But it's all over and I'm here because this big dog here," I pointed to Hannibal deep in sleep, "is going to protect me."

"I think we need to leave town for a while. What has happened to our little Camphor?" Mignon wailed.

"Mignon," I remembered the folder, "I think whoever shot at me might have wanted some information that was in a folder Earlene retrieved from my father's files."

Mignon looked guarded.

"You know what I'm talking about, don't you?" I asked.

"Perhaps. But I think you're wrong about it being connected to the murders."

"Tell me what you know." I was angry that I had been shot at regarding something that Mignon might have warned me about.

"In the late sixties, Brunson Spice had a scandal. Now I don't know what it was, but I do know that it involved a great deal of stock and a loss for the company that year."

"Didn't anyone question what was going on?" I asked.

"Yes, but Horace, whom we all trusted, assured us that it was necessary to transfer the stock and that it must forever be kept quiet."

"It was the sixties and we were all still going to be rich, so we agreed. That's all I know, and I can't imagine what it meant to anyone outside the family."

"I don't get it." I said, feeling my entire body fight the instinct to fall asleep.

"E, you go up to the guestroom and sleep. I'll give Mignon some cake and then we'll tackle this tomorrow." It was nice to see Madge in control for once. Mignon and I agreed with her.

I didn't sleep long. The chocolate cake sat in my rumbling stomach, and the strange sounds of the house confused me. I had fallen asleep in my clothes so I left Howler to sleep on the rug next to the bed and went downstairs. Madge was awake and in the kitchen.

"I thought you'd have been in bed by now." I said pouring a glass of water.

"I'm waiting for Mignon to call," she said, biting the side of her finger.

"Why? Where is she?" I went on alert.

"We were talking about what you'd said, and suddenly she got the idea that she might be able to help—that maybe Maurice knows something. She took Tiffany home and then went to Maurice Brunson's."

"By herself?" I shouted. "Why did you let her go by herself?"

"What's wrong with going to Maurice's? Oh, E, you don't think he is involved in anything?"

"Give me your car keys and call the police. Tell them to go to Maurice's." Maurice's is very close, but it seemed to take forever. I turned my lights off before I pulled into the driveway. Mignon's car wasn't there and the house was entirely dark.

I went around to the back of the house hoping to hide in the shadows. The curtains were pulled so there was no way to see anything. I walked farther to the back where I knew basement windows were exposed. If Mignon was there, perhaps she was trapped down there.

It was dark. I tripped over branches exposed by the roots of the ancient trees that guarded the house. My eyes adjusted enough for me to see the basement entrance and the windows. Please, God, let Madge have called the police. I knelt to look in the windows and at the same time, felt hands choking me. I squirmed, but a deep voice said, "Stop or I will kill you." The hands removed themselves from my throat and pushed me down the basement stairs."

"Well, you did come." With only a candle to light the darkened basement, I saw Glen Newell holding a gun. "Get over with them." I joined a terrified Mignon and a tied up and gagged Maurice."

"She was sneaking around outside Dr. Newell, just like you thought she would." I turned to see a burly-looking man who did odd jobs around town.

"I am so sorry, darling, Mignon hugged me. I suddenly put two and two together and came to have Maurice verify what I remembered about the stock transfer."

I looked at Maurice whose eyes were big as saucers and who was trying to free himself from the gag in his mouth. "Why, Glen? Are you the one who has been terrifying this town?"

Glen Newell was not the nice doctor I knew from the hospital or my parents' parties. "Well, this wasn't my plan," he said, "but it looks like the crazy little Clary girl is going to kill her two friends and then kill herself."

"Were you the one who got the stock transferred?" I wanted to keep Glen Newell talking so he wouldn't wipe us all off the face of the earth.

"Isn't it great! The kid who swept up everyone's dirt in town, finally got what he deserves."

"I can't wait for you to get what you deserve."

"Well, my dear, Mignon, from your tone of voice, I see there really is no fury like a woman scorned. Thanks for the memories."

"Go to hell."

Maurice made only grunts but I could tell he was echoing Mignon's sentiments.

"So what did cause you to become such a monster?" I was out of my head terrified so my mouth seemed to be the only thing working.

"Me? The monster? Let me tell you about monsters. First there's the Nagel group. Clara can't keep her pants on so when she finally gets herself in trouble and tells her father that Philbrook Hanson, a salesman at Brunson, got her pregnant, old man Nagel and Horace

Brunson come to this young intern at the hospital—
me—to perform an abortion. Then to keep me quiet,
they give me beaucoup stock. Sadly, they're not done
with their dastardly deeds. Old Man Nagel hires
somebody to beat the Hansen guy to death and leave
him by the tracks. Again, I'm called in to make it look
like a random act of violence. A young cop named
Harvey Barnes gets paid not to look hard for the guy's
murderer and all's well. For a very long time. My
stock accumulates enough to help me purchase my
place in the Caymans."

"That must have been forty years ago. Why did you
have to murder all those people?" I was in a foggy
place far away from reality.

"Why because little Clara went to Harvey Barnes.
She was feeling guilty. She wanted him to investigate
and right wrongs. Luckily, Harvey was in it up to his
ears, so he told me and I took care of Clara. Then
Harvey got greedy so I had Olaf here," he nodded in the
direction of the handyman, take care of Harvey.
Horace started to panic and think he was next so Olaf
had to take care of him, too."

"Why don't you take that gag out of his mouth," I
looked at Maurice and couldn't stand the gurgling
sounds he was making. "He's no threat."

Glen Newell nodded toward Olaf who jerked the rag
from his mouth.

"I'm sorry E. I thought I could keep all of you from
having to go through this." Maurice's voice was
strained and his body shook.

"No one in town would ever suspect that this jackass
whose id is larger than his brain," Mignon was begging
for trouble, "had the balls to do anything."

"Well, how wrong they were." Newell sneered.
"Poor Glen Newell, the non-Brunson of the group, turns
out to be the smartest of all."

"But you don't need the money," I said. "You've made plenty sitting on boards and you have a steady group of patients."

"Ah but my dear, I also have a steady habit of gambling. Not here, but there are lots of places to gamble not far from here. And I can't stand rich people. If you ask me to give one reason, it would be that I absolute hate the Brunson family. I tried to sell the damn company out from under them but this asshole," he waved his gun at Maurice, "stepped in."

"But I didn't know it was you until I got the file from Caroline's desk. You see, she wasn't pregnant but I distinctly remember John telling me that Glen Newell told her to get rest." Maurice rubbed his obviously sore jaw. "That's when I started to wonder if Glen is who we've always thought he was."

"I can't believe that's the reason she killed herself."

"You're right, Miss Clary, it wasn't. You see, one night Caroline came to the hospital very full of pills and booze. It was then she told me about her manufactured pregnancy and asked me to help. But she also told me something else. She told me that she was the daughter of her father's secretary, not her mother. It seems that her father has always had a roving eye, we shared that, and when he impregnated his secretary, his wife, who couldn't have children, agreed to adopt her. It eventually ruined his wife's life and Caroline's. That snob couldn't stand the thought that she was really just one of the folks."

"So you blackmailed her?" I asked.

"Big time."

"Then did you threaten her?"

"You know, I'm not sure why she did away with herself, except that she was such a controlling witch, I think she couldn't bear the thought that I had power over her. And she knew eventually I would want more than money. She was, after all, a beautiful woman."

"Pig!" Mignon shouted.

"Bitch!" Glen shouted back.

"All this pain and sorrow and for a house in the Caymans"

"For retribution," he grinned maniacally. "I'm off tonight to a place that no one will find me. But I do have loose ends." He turned and shot Olaf between the eyes. "Scream and I'll kill you right now," he said to the three of us.

"Did someone get shot," Madge burst through the basement door. "Oh my god!" she saw Olaf's body and ran to hug me.

"Glen Newell is the murderer," I whispered as Glen stopped to pick up Olaf's gun. I couldn't look at the body. "I see you didn't bring anyone with you," I whispered to Madge.

"Not really. No one answered."

We were all as dead as Olaf.

"Get over there, you enormous pig. I'll have to shoot you all and blame your poor out-of-her-head friend here." He waved the gun at me and gave Madge such a hard shove that she fell down. At that instant something enormous and loud hit Glen Newell, knocking the guns out of his hand and throwing him to the floor.

"See," Madge shouted to us as she grabbed the guns, "I told you he was a watch dog!"

Hannibal might have been up for some praise if he hadn't firmly attached his teeth firmly to a screaming, swearing former Camphor doctor's leg.

"I never thought I would say this, but I love your dog." Mignon said hugging Madge and then the rest of us.

"Well," Javier said as he and Whitey entered the basement, "I see you have things well in control." He pulled Glen Newell to his feet. "Aren't you the clever guy? I'm sure the guys in prison will be glad to have a doctor." He and Whitey led Newell out the door.

"I thought you said you didn't get the police." I hugged Madge again.

"I said no one was there. I didn't say that I didn't leave a message."

"You are brilliant," Maurice embraced Madge in a way that said he regretted not wanting her at the country club.

"There you are," Jory ran down the stairs and into the basement. "When I get done hugging you to death, I'll start biting your head off for doing this." He held me until I breathed normally.

"How did you know?" I asked.

"I called his mother and told her to give him a message." Madge beamed from ear to ear.

"I can't believe that foolish old Glen Newell caused all this trouble." Mignon shook her head.

"Can we really believe it's over?" I asked. "I mean really over.

"I promise you, my love, it is over and you are safe."

I was asleep before Jory drove into my driveway.

Chapter Seventeen

It was hard for me to believe but by the time Christmas rolled around, Camphor had nearly forgotten the activities of the past month. Taylor Brunson hosted the Brunson Christmas party, and everyone praised him for the gracious way he entertained. His uptight wife seemed less uptight, and word was she was becoming a favorite at both the garden and study clubs. As in the years of my childhood at Brunson parties, the children were presented with bountiful Christmas baskets, and chocolate Santas were everywhere.

Mignon had gone to Vi's for the holiday and left Tiffany with her new best friend Madge. It turns out that Hannibal and Tiffany got along much better than their owners and that Tiffany's favorite place to sleep is beside her galumphing friend.

Madge and I were invited to Jory's for Christmas. Mama Esqueda still wasn't crazy about me, but she loved her son, and since his new house had a Viking range that was on back order, she was as gracious a hostess as it was in her to be.

"So, I'll pick you up a little before two and then we'll get Mrs. Bobik, ok?" Jory had said that morning when he stopped over for coffee cake and even sweeter things. "I wanted to give you your present here, though. You said no jewelry—that you don't think we're ready for that, so I've bought you something else." He took out a square package.

"Oh, this is hilarious. It's The Circular Staircase. I love it!" I pulled him to me and loved that he remembered my telling him that the ladies and I never did get to discussing the book.

"It's a first edition, signed by the author," he said. "In a way, it's our song—a great mystery."

"Jory, it's perfect! I'm ashamed that I've not done something that thoughtful for you. It's just a watch." I handed him the gift-wrapped present.

"You said no jewelry. You know I'd love to give you something for your ring finger—take you out of play."

"Open it."

"E, is this your father's?"

"It is. I had the jeweler clean it and check it over. It was a very good watch, and according to Mr. Snyder, it should work another fifty years. I want you to have it. I know my father would, too. It kind of takes you out of play, huh?"

"Definitely."

After a few very special kisses and touches, Jory left to dress and I started upstairs to write. The blinking light reminded me that I had a message.

"Well, E, I have a great present for you." It was Suzi who had surfaced very shortly after Glen Newell's arrest, deciding that this would be her first Christmas as a single lady again. "My friend the editor read *Diabolically Speaking*. She loves the Harriet character, and thinks she can get it published. Merry Christmas, roomy. See you, Jory, and John here for New Year's Eve."

It was Jory's idea to take John along. Oh, he's not ready for anything but friendship, but he and Suzi are old friends so that's a good place to start, right? I think Jory believes in keeping your friends close and your enemies closer. And if down the road, Suzi and John become more than friends, it would work out just fine for all of us. And Earlene and Bryce are indeed expecting their first child. Names? Earlene says if it's a girl, they're partial to Clary. Love it!

Maurice has become an even dearer friend. He spends much more time with Madge and Mignon, feeling that life is too short to forget your real friends. He has even thought, he says, of getting a dog himself. Then we can truly assert that Camphor has gone to the dogs.

Oh, and speaking of dogs, I have to tell you what Mignon gave Madge for Christmas: a mini Hannibal. No kidding. She found a puppy that looks just like Madge's arthritic mutt. Madge was delighted because Mignon said she got it to keep Hannibal young. "I think that means deep down, she really likes him, don't you?" Madge asked me when she introduced me to Caesar— that's his name. I nodded, but I knew it meant that Mignon didn't want Madge to be devastated when Hannibal went to doggie heaven. The ladies love each other more than either of them knows.

And me? Besides loving every minute of getting to know Jory and wondering what job the state police will have him working on next, I write and paint. There's a sequel to *Diabolically Speaking* in the works, and, yes, Harriet and Scrap are making beautiful music together. I also have an idea for a young adult book about a girl named Catherine who suffers from an anxiety disorder. I thought I would call it *Fraidy Cat*. Not bad, huh? But never fear, I'll never give up painting the stately homes in Camphor. After all, that's where my best stories start.

THE END

About The Author

Lyla Fox has three loves: her family, teaching, and writing. She grew up in a small town in Michigan where kids really did play Kick the Can and Hide and Go Seek. They also read Nancy Drew. She credits Nancy for instilling in her a respect for independent women and a love of "sleuthing." Like her character E Clary in *Murder on Cinnamon Street*, Fox is drawn to a good mystery and can't keep herself from investigating. Her son's work in criminal defense, and her daughter's advertising world, provide Fox with fodder for her writing mill. She and her husband Bill divide their time between homes in Kalamazoo, Michigan, and Phoenix, Arizona. She is also the author of *Snoop: A Small Town Gossip Mystery*.